THE AMON WORLD

ABDULWAHID OSMAN

pencil

ISBN 978-93-5667-032-7
© ABDULWAHID OSMAN 2022
Published in India 2022 by Pencil

A brand of

One Point Six Technologies Pvt. Ltd.
123, Building J2, Shram Seva Premises,
Wadala Truck Terminal, Wadala (E)
Mumbai 400037, Maharashtra, INDIA
E connect@thepencilapp.com
W www.thepencilapp.com

Author biography

I'm AbdulWahid Osman and I live in the United Arab Emirates I like to Write stories about Adventures Puzzles Fiction and others. I have a high school certificate and some experience in writing stories because I wrote three stories before. and I also like to read stories related to animes.

CONTENTS

Preface

Traveling to the Amon World was an experience that leaves the youth bewildered. Their Robot partners are suddenly thrust upon them, as well as the concept of having the Robot evolve into stronger creatures, and so the youth have to find out how to be Robot Destined as they go along. They quickly learn of the Amon World's plight, and how evil Robots are intent on ruling it for themselves. Although they originally fight just to return home, they eventually vow to save the Amon World for the sake of their Robot friends. As the plot evolves, the youth deal with various aspects of maturity: making friends, being courageous, standing for one's morals, etc. Each youth receives an object called a "Star" that embodies a particular trait that defines them, and whose power could be used to evolve their partners to the next level. Tom has Courage, Mark has Friendship, Sarah has Love, Maria has Sincerity, Kevin has Knowledge, Jack has Reliability, and Thomas has Hope. It is later revealed that the youth were chosen to become Destined and that their Stars represent the positive personality traits that they most strongly evinced at that time.Eventually, an army of evil Robots led by Martin crossed through a dimensional gate from the Amon World to enter Earth. The Youth and their partners followed. Specifically, they landed in Okon, the youth's hometown. As the youth battled on Earth, they were joined by an eighth member, Kate, Tom's sister and carrier of the trait of Light. While this was happening, a group of four Mega-level Robots called the Dark Robots besieged the Amon World. Once things were taken care of on Earth, the eight youth returned to the Amon World once again in order to defeat the Dark Robots one by one, and eventually their real enemy, Albert, the Robot who made all of the evil Robots the Youth had previously destroyed. When Albert was defeated, the youth went back to the Real World, leaving their Robot partners behind.

The begins...

Tom recounts how the world's climate has been going haywire—Africa is in a drought, Asia is being hit by flash floods, and Europe is wracked with freezing cold temperatures. Meanwhile, he's in summer camp, having a perfectly normal summer until it begins snowing, and a sudden blizzard appears. Tom and his friends, Sarah, Mark, Kevin, Maria, Thomas, and Jack, are all amazed when it begins snowing. They then observe lights like auroras in the sky, from which emerges a portal that shoots out strange electronic devices. When they reach out and grab the objects, a huge wave of water erupts from the ground and sucks them into the portal, which sends them to a new world. Tom is awoken by a robot that calls itself Kane, and soon Kevin shows up with his own robot, Max. The robots claim to know Tom and Kevin and to have been waiting a long time for them. The youths try to figure out where they are, and Tom climbs a tree to take a look through his telescope. He's startled to find that they are near the sea and then spots a huge black beetle which Kane tells him is Robot Beetle. It attacks Tom and Kevin, but they hide within a "hiding tree", which is partially a hologram. After the robot beetle passes, Sarah tells them to come out, and the group is reunited and introduced to each youth's new robot. Sarah has Yoko. Thomas has Terry whom he instantly hits it off. Mark has Troy. Jack has Bobby whom he is afraid of. The robots then explain that they are "Amon: Amon Robots!".As the group wonders where Maria is, they hear her screaming and spot her and her Tiffany being chased by Robot Beetle. It chases the gang to the edge of a cliff, and the Robot decides to fight despite the youth wanting to flee. However, as In-Training robots, they can only blow bubbles and are knocked out by the Champion-level Robot Beetle. The youth tries to stop them from fighting, and just as everything seems lost, the devices glow and the Robots suddenly evolve to Rookie-level! Kane becomes Kane 2, Yoko becomes Yoko 2, Max becomes Max 2, Troy becomes Troy 2, Terry becomes Terry 2, Bobby becomes Bobby 2, and Tiffany becomes Tiffany 2. While the humans are shocked by the transformation, the seven Rookie robots begin attacking the robot beetle, but even their combined attacks are only enough to daze it. It crashes into the cliff, breaking off the chunk the youths and Robots are on and letting it fall into the river.

Against a Shell Robot at the beach

The seven Youths and their Robots fall from the outcropping that Beetle Robot had dislodged, and although each Robot attempts to grab the humans, it is Bobby 2 and his "Marching Robots" that are able to catch the humans by forming a raft. The youths arrive at the shore and discover that their in-training pals are now in rookie form because they have evolved. The new Robot introduces itself and explains to the youths that they were able to evolve because they shared energy with their partners. The youths try to figure out where they are and what to do next. Tom tells the group that he saw a beach and sea. The group follows him while Jack protests that they should stay put until the grown-ups come to get them. While walking, the youths start to get acquainted with their Robot. They arrive at the beach and discover many telephone offices and try them. However only weird facts and nonsense are heard from the phones. The youths then rest and are very hungry. They each take out what they have. Unfortunately, in the food category, they only have Thomas's snacks and emergency rations from Jack. They also rediscover the little devices on their pants or bags. Jack then splits the food but it can only be good for a day with the Robot. The Robot says that they are alright and that they can manage for themselves however Tom still gives some food to Kane 2. Suddenly Shell robot appears and is very angry that the youths are on his territory. He begins to attack them. So the seven chosen Robots attempt to fight the Shell robot, but none of their attacks work besides Kane 2's since he ate and the rest are hungry. The other Robots are not able to fight. Tom helps by making a diversion. Then Shell robot grabs Tom and traps Kane 2 under his paw. Right, when the Shell robot is going to attack everyone else, Tom's Device glows and Kane 2 evolves to Kane 3. Shell robot drops Tom, and the two champion levels fight. Kane 3 defeats Shell's robot, blasting him through the air and into the sea. Kane 3 reverts back to Kane 2 who is now exhausted and hungry. The youths quickly feed their Robots. Jack is still trying to use the phone offices but they are all smashed. They all realize the Shell robot isn't dead and could still come back. They need to leave. The group then heads off, ready for whatever Robot may be out there to fight!.

The Troy 3!

Tom asks Kane 2 why he doesn't just stay in his Kane 3 form because he thought it was really cool. Kane 2 tells him that he can't because it uses too much energy. Suddenly, a Rhino Robot comes out of nowhere and attacks. Then another one appears! The Youths run away as the two Robot fight. When the sun begins to set, the group realizes that they are tired. Mark wants to keep walking because they don't know if it's safe to stop, but Tom says they need food. Max 2 finds a lake for them to camp at. They find an empty trolley car there and decide to stay in it. Now that they have shelter, the group just needs food. The youths and their partners all go to gather things to eat for dinner. Tom starts to realize that Mark doesn't really treat Thomas like a brother. It's much more like he's a bother. Sarah agrees with him. As Jack looks in the sky to figure out where they are, he finds that he doesn't recognize any constellations. He can't even find the north star. Tom suggests that they could be in the southern hemisphere. Everyone is getting very tired and is ready to go to sleep but Kevin thinks that they should take turns standing guard. Tom says that they can all do it for an hour but Mark says Thomas is too young and needs sleep. He then starts to get in a fight with Tom for bothering Troy 2. Jack finally decides that the order will be Tom, Mark, Kevin, and Jack. Everyone else can go sleep in the trolley.

While they're sleeping, Mark has Troy 2 go sleep by Thomas to keep him warm. During his turn, Tom notices that Mark is up too. Mark apologizes and says that it's stressful being in the Amon World and watching Thomas. Tom asks if they even live in the same house and Mark explains that their parents are divorced and he lives with their dad while Thomas is with their mom. After Tom says that that explains a lot, Mark runs away to a nearby island. Then Tom and Kane 2 hear Mark playing his harmonica. Troy 2 hears it too and comes to join his partner. While Tom and Kane 2 are sitting by the fire, it begins to spark and the ground shakes. The sparks have hit the tail of a Sea snake Robot and he's mad. He pulls away from the island everyone else is on leaving just Mark and Troy 2 on their separate one. The Robot tries to fight Sea Snake Robot but is not strong enough. Kane 2 also doesn't have the strength to evolve. Mark and Troy 2 have now jumped in the water to distract Sea snake Robot but he grabs Mark. As he is in trouble his Device begins to glow and Troy 2 evolves to Troy 3! Troy 3 frees Mark and defeats Sea snake Robot. Bobby 2 has his robot friends bring the island back to the mainland. The Youths then discover that their Robots can only evolve when they are in trouble like how Mark was in trouble or when Tom and Kane 2 evolved. Everyone is very tired after an exciting night and all fall asleep except for Mark and Tom. Tom hears Mark's harmonica again and sees him playing for his sleeping brother and their partners. Tom watches as Mark plays and Thomas sleeps with a smile on his face.

The Fire Mountain

The Youths are wandering through a forest full of signs (Mark calls it the Forest of Irrelevant Road Signs) when they see a strange Red Star in the sky. They start to wonder what it is and where they are. Tom says that they have to keep moving after stopping when Thomas trips. Sarah agrees and says that they all need to stay together and use teamwork to figure out where they are (despite everyone walking away as she says this). Mark sees a bunch of telephone poles and says they should follow them. At the same time, Kevin sees the Red Star again crashing into Fire Mountain. As they are following the poles, the youths realize that they have no wires connecting them. They are then reminded of the phone offices and the trolley car. They also notice other weird things such as Maria's compass not working. Everyone is very hot and tired when Tom spots water. They see it's in a village and head in its direction. Meanwhile, the red star they saw earlier embeds itself into a Fire Robot. When the Youths get to the village, they see that it is completely inhabited by Yoko 1. Yoko 1 asks Yoko 2 all about how she evolved. Yoko 2 tells them that it's because of the bond she shares with Sarah and how she needed to protect her human partner. The Yoko 1 invites everyone to have dinner with them and they also go to the fountain for water. Suddenly, the fountain starts to erupt lava. The lake is empty too. The youths think that the sudden drought could have something to do with the Red Star they saw hitting the mountain where the water comes from. While getting a better look through his telescope, Tom sees Fire Robot heading for them. He's in great pain and burning even though he's made of fire. As Fire Robot gets closer, everyone begins to run away and hide in a boat in the dried-up lake. Yoko 2 stays behind to help Yoko 1 and Sarah goes after her. Just then Fire Robot attacks Yoko 2 but Sarah saves her. Since they are still in danger, Yoko 2 goes back to fight! Her rookie attacks don't do anything and when the other Robot comes, their attacks only make him bigger as Fire Robot cries out in pain. Yoko 2 realizes that her friends are in danger and evolves to Yoko 3. The two fight and after getting a good hit on Fire Robot, the Red Star comes out of his back. They realize that's what was making him crazy. Then Yoko 3 turns back into Yoko 2 and hugs Sarah. The Yoko 1 asks Fire Robot why he attacked their village and he tells them he couldn't control himself and the last thing he remembers was being hit by the Red Star. They are just happy that he's better and Fire Robot goes back to the mountain. After that, everyone eats the dinner they were promised. All the Robots love it but the youths are a little reluctant to eat the seeds they are given despite there being more than enough for seconds.

The Strange Factory

The youth and their partners are all very tired from wandering around and Kevin's laptop still won't work. Tom tries hitting it and Kevin gets mad. Tai sees smoke in the distance and he and Kane 2 go to see what it is. Kevin finally gets his computer working but unfortunately, the battery is low. Tai calls everyone else over and they see the smoke is from a factory. The youths go to investigate it but find the factory to be abandoned. There are however lots of machines putting things together by themselves. Everyone splits up into two groups. The group of Tom, Kane 2, Sarah, Yoko 2, Jack, and Bobby 2 find an Iron Robot stuck under a machine. They are able to free him but at the same time, a Red Star gets stuck in his leg. He wakes up and begins to attack. Kane 2 blasts the roof above Iron Robot and it collapses on top of him. The group then runs away. Meanwhile, Kevin, Max 2, Mark, Troy 2, Maria, Tiffany 2, Thomas, and Terry 2 find a giant battery that powers the whole factory. Kevin tries to figure out how it works as the others watch the machines. Kevin and Max 2 find a way inside the battery which is full of codes. Kevin erases some of it and the factory loses all of its power. When Kevin rewrites the code, the power comes back. Meanwhile, Iron Robot has gotten free and is chasing Tom's group. Kevin is still trying to decode the inscriptions in the battery. Max 2 wonders why Kevin would rather spend time with puzzles than with people. Kevin says it's because he thinks it is fun to try and figure things out. He wants to know how they all got to the Amon World and what the Robot is. Max 2 says he still doesn't understand Kevin and asks if there is a deep dark secret he's hiding. Kevin remembers a conversation that he overheard his parents having. Suddenly, the text on Kevin's computer starts to jumble and his Device starts to glow. The machines that Mark's group is watching start to take the things they are building apart. Kevin has unlocked something on his computer but Max 2 starts burning and glowing. Kevin disconnects the program and Max 2 gets better. Iron Robot is about to get Tom's group when Tom grabs him with a crane and he is stuck as they run away. Everyone comes back together but Iron Robot has gotten free and finds them. He shoots missiles that are about to hit Thomas but Troy 3 saves him. Then the missiles aim for everyone else and Kane 3 joins Troy 3. Unfortunately, the two champions can't beat the ultimate. Then Kevin puts the program back into his computer and Max 2 evolves to Max 3. Max 3 destroys the Red Star by aiming for Iron Robot's right leg and Iron Robot becomes good again. Then he helps the youths get out of the factory by going through the sewers. Once in the sewers, Tom and Kane 2 try to hit Kevin's computer again, but Kevin simply moves out of the way so they hit each other.

The Rainbow Town

The Youth are wandering through the sewers with their partners and singing. Sarah becomes very emotional upon remembering when she used to sing at home when hanging laundry out to dry and how much she misses it. Tom says that he misses playing sports followed by a hot bath. Thomas. misses video games Mark misses steak, Jack misses doing his homework, Maria misses the beach, and Kevin misses looking at the stars and planets. The youths are interrupted from their thoughts when they hear a pack of Sewer Robots coming toward them. They all run as sludge is thrown at them by the Sewer Robot, though they soon escape through an opening in the sewer because the Sewer Robots don't like sunlight. The youths wander for a while when they see a bunch of vending machines. Despite thinking it's a trick like the phone offices they recently saw, Maria tries one anyway. After putting money in the machine, a Sewer Robot comes out and it has a crush on Maria. She rejects him and he gets mad, but Maria is not worried because the sun is out. Just then, the clouds cover the sun and another pack of Sewer robots come out and chase the youths again. They decide to split up. Right before Tiffany 2 attacks the Sewer robot chasing her and Maria, the Sewer robot runs away. It is because there is a Rat Robot behind them. He is usually a nice Robot who runs Sewer Town but he starts chasing them. Maria and

Tiffany 2 escape after running into the Sewer Robot that likes Maria. After turning him down again, they figure that something must be wrong in Sewer Town and so they head there. Maria and Tiffany 2 arrive at the Rainbow town and see all of the other Youth running around with the toys saying they are having fun. However, they don't sound like they're having fun. Maria and Tiffany 2 then find a locked chest that is full of all the other Robot partners. Kane 2 tells them they had been captured by Rat Robot. Maria and Tiffany 2 then go off to fight Rat Robot alone. As he is attacking them, the Sewer robots come to their rescue, or at least they try to. They are easily defeated. Tiffany 2 goes to join them in the fight. Then she evolves into Tiffany 3 who defeats Rat Robot, causing a Red Star to come out of his back. Everyone is freed and Rat Robot apologizes. He then gives them all a big hug as Maria once again turns down the Sewer Robots.

The Glacier Mountain

The Youth and their partners are wandering through a cold forest. They are discussing all of the fun things they could do in the snow when Jack tells them they need to be more serious and safe but everyone else laughs and thinks Jack should lighten up. They find themselves at a field covered with snow and try to decide between crossing it or climbing the nearby Glacier Mountain. Before a discussion is reached, the youths smell something and see steam. After following the steam, they find a bunch of pools filled with boiling water. There is also a refrigerator filled with nothing but eggs. Jack doesn't think they should eat them but everyone else is hungry and disagrees. As everyone enjoys their feast of eggs, they start to feel homesick. The youths feel better after talking about their favorite kinds of eggs but Jack just gets annoyed. Everyone thinks he is acting weird and should lighten up but Jack says he is just being careful because nobody else will and he needs to be the voice of reason. Tom and Mark are fighting over whether or not to climb Glacier Mountain. Tom says it would give them a great view of the whole island but Mark says it would be too dangerous and they don't know what's up there. As Jack goes to break up the fight, they try to make him take sides. Unfortunately, he sees valid points in both of their arguments. The youths finally decide to go to bed and figure it out in the morning, but Jack is worried that he is not being responsible enough as the oldest to take care of everyone. In the middle of the night, he and Bobby 2 go off on their own to climb Glacier Mountain. After getting halfway up the mountain, it starts to shake violently. Red Stars start to appear at the top of it. As Jack and Bobby 2 go to see where the stars are coming from, an Owl Robot flies over them. Bobby 2 is about to go over and talk to him when a star comes from the sky and embeds itself into Owl's back. He then starts to attack. Meanwhile, Sarah wakes up and finds that Jack is gone. She thinks he went up Glacier Mountain and woke up everybody else. As the owl robot is about to unleash an attack on Jack and Bobby 2, Yoko 3 shows up with Sarah, Tom, and Kane 2. Owl robot defeats Yoko 3 so Kane 2 evolves to Kane 3, but he is defeated too. To protect his friends, Jack jumps onto Owl's robot back to try to pull out the star. He can't do it and he falls off. Just then, Bobby 2 evolves to Bobby 3 and catches Jack. He is also able to destroy the star. Jack, Tom, Sarah, Bobby 2, Kane 2, and Yoko 2 then make their way to the top of Glacier Mountain. Upon getting there, they see that beyond the island is nothing but water.

The Strange Mansion

As the youths come to terms with being stuck on an island in the middle of nowhere, a brave Robot by the name of a Lion robot, who is also on Glacier Mountain, is attacked by his arch-rival, a Bear robot. However, the fight is soon broken up by Dragon Robot, one of the evilest Robots of all. He informs them of the Youth's presence on the mountain and orders them to work together to eliminate them. Whilst the bear's robot's only objection is to working with the Lion robot, the Lion robot is completely against the idea, and attempts to strike the Dragon robot, who strikes the Lion robot in response, taking control of him in the process. Meanwhile, Tom is attempting to draw a map of the island, despite the comments of the other youths on his poor map-making skills. At that moment, the Lion robot appears and, much to the surprise of the other Robot, proceeds to destroy the group. Whilst making their escape, Tom drops his map. He goes back for it, and Kane 2 fires a to defend him, which ends up burning the map. Soon, the way is blocked by the Bear robot, and the group is left with no choice but to stand and fight. The Robots change to their Champion forms and manage to hold off the enemy until the Dragon robot causes a landslide above, distracting them and giving the Bear robot and Lion robot the chance to retreat. Once the dust settles, the youths find their Robot back in their Rookie forms, tired and hungry.

Whilst searching for a decent place to rest, they come across a mansion, of all things, and decide to investigate. They discover a feast laid out in the dining room, and are soon helping themselves. As the sun goes down, the youths and their Robot have a relaxing bath before settling down in bed. Everyone quickly falls asleep, allowing Dragon Robot and his two servants to sneak into the mansion unnoticed. However, Tom and Kane 2 are soon making their way to the bathroom. As they're about to head back to bed, the Bear robot jumps out from hiding, and they hurry to escape, before running into the Lion robot. At that point, the Dragon robot reveals himself to Tom and Kane 2, and the mansion turns out to be an illusion. As the rest of the group awakens to this reality, the Dragon robot proceeds to eliminate them, raising their beds into the air. At the same time, the island begins to be torn apart by the Dragon robot's Red stars. Kane 2 soon realizes that he doesn't have the strength to fight against the Lion robot, having eaten no real food at all, and Tom is soon in the Lion robot's grip. Tom's bed then crashes nearby, and his device falls out, shining a bright light that frees Lion robot of Dragon's robot control. Lion robot then fires a blow at the Dragon robot, distracting him from the other youths, who are sent flying off in all directions. But before the Lion robot can attack again, the Bear robot appears, and so he's left with no choice but to send Tom and Kane 2 away, as he is once again taken over by the Dragon robot. Now the youths are separated, and the island continues to drift further and further apart.

The Ice Robot

Still, on the block of ice, Tom and Kane 2 find some land. Tom is still in his blue briefs. Tom soon finds his clothes (which are frozen, so he has Kane 2 warm them up), and after he's dressed he tries to see where the other parts of the island are going. At that moment, an Ice robot attacks the two. Kane 2 and Tom try to avoid his attacks and find a Red Star in his back. Tom has Kane 2 roll up into a football ball and kicks him onto the Ice robot's back and Kane 2 burns the Red star, reverting the Ice robot to his nicer self. Tom asks him if he saw any other youths like him. He tells the two that he saw a youth with a Troy 2, but the island he landed on is going by quickly. Since Tom and Kane 2 helped him, the Ice robot makes an ice bridge to walk across and the three start walking. On the Island, Mark and Troy 2 are walking in a snowstorm to find the others, and Mark starts to get cold, so Troy 2 finds a cave for them to stay in. Mark goes along thinking Thomas must be in there, but when he finds it empty he wants to go back out. Troy 2 starts a fire and says he will go find Thomas. When Mark becomes impatient, he goes back into the storm, but after a short while he passes out. Troy 2 finds him unconscious and brings him back to the cave, keeping him warm with his fur. The next day Tom, Troy 2, and the Ice robot arrive at the island and begin searching for Mark and the Ice robot. Meanwhile, Mark wakes up and thanks Troy 2, who now has Mark's cold. Tom and Kane 2 soon find the two, and the Ice robot goes off to find some food. Mark and Tom get into an argument about what they should do next. Mark wants to search for the others, but Tom thinks they should head back to Glacier Mountain and reminds Mark that the others were on different islands and the islands are too far apart. A fight soon breaks out, and the two end up rolling towards a cliff edge. Mark then expresses his worries for Thomas, but before Tom can respond, the cliff they're both on crumbles away. With Mark and Tom hanging for their life by a branch, and their Robot too tired to help, all hope seems lost. Then Penguin Robot appears to knock them down. Fortunately, their fall is broken by the Ice robot, who's just come back with food and medicine. The robots are now able to evolve and are able to free the Penguin robot of the Red star in his chest. They then find some Red Stars within the cliff face broken down during the fight and destroying them causes the island to begin moving back to Glacier Mountain. The two youths forget their troubles and look toward their next plan of action.

Kevin and Maria in the temple

Kevin, Max2, Maria, and Tiffany 2 are all plummeting through the sky in their beds and are about to crash. Maria and Tiffany 2 find themselves in a forest while Kevin and Max 2 are outside of some ancient ruins which Kevin, much to his partner's protests, decides to investigate. As Maria and Tiffany 2 are wandering through the forest, they run into Sam and Cole who start to attack them after Maria insults the two. They see Maria's Device in her bag and Sam was about to grab it when a light came from it making them leave the girls alone. They also say they saw another human with a Max 2 land by the ruins and will take Maria and her partner there. Unfortunately, it is on a different island. Tiffany 2 uses her poison ivy to get to the other island and Sam and Cole ask for a goodbye. the two tell them they'll wait. Meanwhile, Kevin and Max 2 are in the ruins and they find a large spinning Red Star and lots of writing on the walls. Kevin recognizes it as being the same writing they saw in the giant battery. At the same time, Maria and Tiffany 2 have arrived at the temple and run into the others. Kevin barely even cares because he is so preoccupied with his computer and the writing in the ruins. Maria tries to get him to go look for everyone else but he doesn't care. Kevin finally figures out the code and a maze pops up on his computer. Maria gets so upset that Kevin is ignoring her that she runs away crying and Max 2 follows while Tiffany 2 is still crying. As Maria runs through the maze with Max 2 hot on her trail, Kevin and Tiffany 2 try to figure out where they are. As Maria realizes that she and Max 2 are lost, Tiffany 2 wants to go into the maze after them but Kevin tries to crack the maze first and he is able to find where they are through her Device. With them, they can communicate and Kevin can tell Maria how to get out. As he is doing this, someone else appears on his map and starts to follow Maria and Max 2. It's Horse Robot being controlled by a red star. He starts chasing them and when asked for directions on where to go after hitting a dead end, Kevin and Tiffany 2 are gone from Kevin's computer. Robot Horse catches them and shoots a hole in the wall. Maria tells Max 2 to evolve, but he can't because Kevin's not there. Just then, Tiffany 2 and Kevin arrive. As the partners have been reunited, both robots are able to evolve and destroy the Red Star. Horse Robot sees the Device on Maria's bag and tells them that the ruins are its temple and he is its guardian. He explains that the Device is the preserver of light and the last line of defense against darkness. Then the Lion robot shows up and says he will destroy the youth. The horse robot says he must protect them because they possess the Devices, but the Lion robot is able to beat him. Right as he is about to attack, Kevin and Maria's Devices begin to glow and the Lion robot runs away. Kevin goes back to cracking the code in the writing from the wall and Maria gets so frustrated that she kicks the giant red star. It then starts to rotate the other way and the moving island they are on starts moving back towards Glacier Mountain.

The Ghost Robot

Jack and Bobby 2 are floating through the sea on a bed. Jack starts to freak out because Bobby 2 is eating all of the food and he is seasick. Then a giant crate floats over to the bed and the Bear robot is inside of it. He begins to attack them with his club. Bobby 2 calls in his army of fish but even with so many of them, they can't stop Bobby 2. As he is about to attack Jack, Bobby 2 evolves into Bobby 3, who is able to escape with Jack on his back. Unfortunately, he is tired and hungry and turns back into Bobby 2 and the two start to sink. Meanwhile, Sarah is fishing and hooks something big. When she pulls it up, it turns out to be Jack and Bobby 2. Jack is unconscious and Booby 2 explains to Sarah and Yoko 2 what happened. He also says that he is worried about Jack's self-confidence after what happened and to get it back, they should make Jack their leader. Jack then wakes up and is shocked to find out they want him to lead them. He is finally convinced and embraces his new position. Then they hear bells and the group sees a church in the distance. Jack takes them there and he goes in to find a group of people in masks dancing. He gets everyone else and they are shocked to see other humans. One of them comes and takes Jack's group inside. He says that they are celebrating the "Ghost holiday" and would love to have them all as guests. Bobby 2 asks the man why they honor Ghost robot because he is a Bad Robot. The man gets very mad and reveals that he and everyone else are Ghost robots! Jack's group is surrounded and Bobby 2 and Yoko 2 are too hungry to evolve. They are then all kidnapped by the Ghost robots. Jack and Sarah are tied up to be eaten by the Ghost robots while Bobby 2 and Yoko 2 are thrown in a jail cell. They realize that to escape, they must trick the guard. He had been sleeping but Bobby 2 woke him by throwing a rock. He and Yoko 2 tell him he is bad at being evil because he is not taunting them. The Ghost robot says he doesn't know how and his prisoners explain that he must find out what they want and get it but not let them have it. They tell him they are hungry and he should get food but not give it to them. The Ghost robots get some fruits and Bobby 2 and Yoko 2 trick him into coming so close that they beat him up and eat the food. At the same time, Jack and Sarah are about to be eaten as the Ghost robots all combine into one huge one. When it is about to get them, their partners show up and evolve. As Bobby 3 and Yoko 3 fight the giant Ghost robot, Jack and Sarah run and hide behind some gravestones. The ghost robot is winning but Jack is determined to help their partners beat him. He starts saying a chant to get the Ghost robot to lose his power and starts hitting Sarah's beanie to a rhythm. The ghost robot then starts to shrink and Bobby 3 and Yoko 3 are able to beat him! The ground then opens to reveal many Red Stars which all break apart. They then start to head back to Glacier Mountain.

The Toy Town

After Thomas and Terry 2 land after their bed crashes, Thomas starts to be sad because he misses the other Youth. Terry 2 is sad that he can't evolve to help Thomas and he is sad too. Thomas wants to know what Terry 2 will become but he doesn't know yet until it happens. Thomas imagines that it could be something like a pig. This makes Terry 2 mad as he insists that he is not a pig. The two then start to wander and find themselves in Toy Town. They have a great time playing in the Town but then they find a bunch of cradles full of baby Robots. There are also many robots-Eggs. Terry 2 finds a note by one that says rub me so Thomas rubs one of the eggs which hatches into a Robot. They want to go find a cradle for it but one magically appears. The two partners then discuss not being able to remember when they were babies, though Thomas does recall a time when Mark helped him when he was sad. Meanwhile, Guard robot, the caretaker of Toy Town is having very good luck fishing. Unfortunately, Thomas and Terry 2 are having much less luck with the baby Robot who are all crying. When the Guard robot gets back he attacks Thomas and Terry 2 because he thinks they are hurting the babies. Guard robot tells them they must leave but Terry 2 refuses and the two begin to fight. Thomas finally intervenes and makes them stop. He has them have a Tug-O-War instead. It is intense, but Terry 2 ends up winning. Afterward, the two Robots become friends, surrounded by the jubilant infants, and the Guard robot apologizes for acting harshly. He invites them to stay for a while. Thomas accepts but also asks how to get to Glacier Mountain. Guard robot says it's very dangerous and they will have to fight the Dragon robot. Thomas says he doesn't want to fight. He just wants to be friends with people and laugh with them. Then Guard robot gets an idea that the power of friendship might be able to fix the island. Thomas thinks maybe his team can get back together. Dragon robot has been watching and he wants to destroy Thomas and Terry 2 before he can evolve. He sends the Lion robot out to do it. Meanwhile, Thomas and Terry 2 have been playing with the baby Robot. Thomas and Terry 2 promise to always be best friends and everybody cheers but the Lion robot is lurking not too far away, getting ready to strike.

The Terry 3

As Thomas and Terry 2 play with the baby Robot in Toy Town, Lion Robot arrives to attack them. The two go and hide but they run into Bear Robot. Lion Robot then catches up to them. As he is about to kill Thomas, Mark, Troy 3, Tom, and Kane 3 show up to save them. As the four champion-level Robots are fighting, more Red Stars embed themselves into the Lion robot which becomes huge and more evil and powerful. He easily defeats Troy 3 and Kane 3. Terry 2's attacks do nothing against him. Just then, Kevin, Max 3, Maria and Tiffany 3 come. Kevin and Maria inform the others that their Devices have the power to destroy Red Stars. Tom and Mark shine them on Lion Robot who turns back to normal while Max3 drives off Bear Robot. Lion Robot tells the youths that legends say that a group of youth called the Champions will come to the Amon World and save it from the darkness. He knows it is them because they can evolve their partners. Kevin predicts that after saving the Amon World they will be able to go home. The group then sets off to defeat Dragon Robot. However, the Dragon robot is not worried as he sends out more Red Stars. Sarah, Yoko 3, Jack, and Bobby 3 see them on their way to Glacier Mountain. Tom's group has reached the peak of the mountain when suddenly Dragon Robot appears. Right after, Sarah's group does too. The Robot with the ability to all evolve and the six of them along with the Lion robot begin to fight Dargon Robot but they have no effect on the powerful Robot. Thomas and Terry 2 stand by helplessly as Dragon Robot is about to get them. The others try to save them but can't. As Dragon Robot grabs the two, a light starts shining from his hand. Terry 2 has evolved to Terry 3! Dragon Robot is still not worried but Terry 3 says that he will destroy Dragon Robot and bring peace. He gathers energy from all of the Devices which causes everyone to evolve except for him who is now more powerful. He sends a strong blast right through the evil Robot. Dargon Robot is destroyed but he is telling Terry 3 that there will be eviler and he has used up all of his energy too. For that reason, he is also dying. As Thomas cries, Terry 3 uses the last of his energy to tell him that he will come back. His feathers then come together to form a Robot Egg which Thomas hugs and vows to take care of as the others assure him that it is Terry 2. The island then starts to reform as the darkness has been defeated. As the youths wonder why they are not going home, they realize there must be more evil they have to fight. Suddenly, Gerard appears as a hologram, to the surprise of the youth.

The Simon Continent

Gerard explains to the Youth and their partners that he is talking to them in the form of a hologram from the Simon Continent. He does not know how they can get home but he still needs their help in defeating other evil Robots. They will need to evolve once more to the next level. To do so, the youths will need to find the Tags and Crests. The Crests are scattered throughout Simon Continent but the Tags were hidden by the Dragon robot. Gerard's hologram then disappears but not before being able to put a map on Kevin's computer. The youths wonder how to get to Simon Continent, which is very far away according to Kevin's map. Most of the group doesn't think it is a good idea to go but Thomas says they should so they all agree. The next day, everyone begins to build a raft. Lion robot shows up with Horse robot, Guard robot, Penguin robot, Rat robot, Ice robot, Fire robot, and the Yoko 2 to help. With their help, the raft gets finished in no time. Just then, Thomas's Robot-Egg hatches into a Terry! He is thrilled and with that, the youth and their partners leave File Island to go to Simon Continent with all of their friends saying goodbye. As the group is sailing, a giant tidal wave comes. It was caused by a Whale Robot who eats them. After being sent down the esophagus where they are attacked by antibodies, they end up in the stomach which is quickly filling up with stomach acid. As they are looking for a way out, Sarah spots a Red Star in Whale Robot. Tiffany 2 uses her "Poison Ivy" to latch onto the Red Star. Tom climbs it and uses his Device to destroy the Red Star. Whale Robot then shoots the raft out through his blow hole and apologizes to everyone. As their raft is now broken, Whale Robot offers to take the group to Simon Continent. He also says that he once saw Dragon Robot hide something deep in the ocean and will take the youths there to see what it was. They end up in a cove and when Whale Robot lets them off, the group sees a convenience store but they run into a Seal Robot with a Red Star before they can reach it. Bobby 2 evolves into Bobby 3 to fight Seal Robot while everyone else looks for the tags. They go into the store but it's being destroyed. Max 2 then joins the fight by evolving to Max 3 and he is able to break the Gear. In all the scuffles, Thomas loses Terry. When he finds him, Terry has a box. It contains the Tags. Now that they have them, the youths just need the Crests so they continue onto Simon Continent with Whamon to get them.

The Eagle Robot

Everyone is sleeping on Whale Robot except for Tom who is getting impatient. Luckily, out in the distance, he spots Simon Continent. He wakes everyone up and they are all excited to arrive. Whale Robot wishes them luck on finding the Crests and leaves. He had however told the group about a Kane Village that they could go to. Kane 2 smells the Kane as he used to be one and they follow his nose into a forest where they find a village. However, in the village, all they find are Pigeon robots. They carry Maria who had run ahead and the group runs after her. When everyone catches up, they find Maria happily taking a bath. Unfortunately, Tom and Kevin run in on her, infuriating Maria, and their brief moment of panic quickly turns to embarrassment. The Pigeon robots happily welcome the Youth and their partners with food but Kane 2 knows that what he smelled was Kane and he and Troy 2 agree that there is something wrong here, along with a few of the others. While eating. That night while the group is sleeping, the Pigeon Robots kidnaps Terry. They run into some Rabbit Robots who want to know where Terry came from. They tell them he was with a group of humans and then put Terry in a cage in a cave behind a waterfall. One of the Rabbit Robots leaves to tell Eagle Robot that the Youth have arrived. Eagle robot is upset to learn that the youths got to Simon's continent sooner than he thought they would so he unleashes his dark network. Meanwhile, everyone is searching for Terry. As Kane 2 is looking in the forest, he smells Kane again. His nose leads him to the waterfall where he finds the cave behind it and a captive Terry along with many Kane. They tell Kane 2 that the Pigeon robots came and locked them up so they could take over the village. As he is going to free the prisoners, some Rabbit robots appear and attack Kane 2. He then starts shooting his pepper breath through the waterfall to make a smoke signal which Tai sees. Everyone is about to go look when the Pigeon robot starts telling them not to. They realize that the Pigeon robots lied to them all and they run away. Tom arrives just in time to save Kane 2 who evolves into Kane 3. He easily defeats the Rabbit robots in one shot and the Youth free Terry and the Kane robots. But as everything seems fine, Eagle Robot arrives. He uses his dark network and starts to destroy the village. Troy 2 evolves to Troy 3 but before anyone else can, the dark network makes them not evolve. They realize that the only way to beat Eagle Robot is to evolve to the next level as Gerard said. They are all trapped in the cave when Tom's tag begins to glow as well as the whole room. The wall disappears and becomes Tom's Crest of Courage. The group is able to escape through the hole but Eagle Robot is not worried as he is sure he will be able to find the youths.

The SkullKane

The Youth and their partners are wandering through the desert and they are getting very tired and are also starting to lose hope. Tom tells them that everything will be okay because they have a crest. He starts to pressure Kane 2 into evolving. Tom wonders how Kane 2 will be able to evolve again. Kevin explains that if it works the same way as before, Kane 2 will need to have lots of energy from food and Tom will need to be in danger. Tom then starts stuffing all of the food that the group has into Kane 2 despite him being full. Everyone else begins to worry about Kane 2 and also Tom's personality changing. Sarah recalls that when they used to play for the same football team, Tom did everything he could to help the team and is currently doing the same now, Suddenly, Jack's tag begins to glow. As they wonder where the crest is, Tom sees something out in the distance. Jack heads there, thinking it must be where his crest is when he trips over a cable buried in the sand. Meanwhile, Eagle's Robot computer tells him that the youths are near the Castle. He then calls one of his Rabbit Robots who is stationed there to be ready for them. The youth and their partners arrive at the Castle but are confused that it has football goals. Tom tells everyone to split up and look for Jack's crest but Kane 2 falls over needing to rest from all the food Tom made him eat. Jack tells everyone to rest while he and Bobby 2 look but Tom follows to look too. A football then rolls over to the group and Sarah organizes a game for them all. Tom angrily kicks the ball away and yells at everyone for playing a game now. As Jack's tag starts to glow even brighter, Eagle Robot appears. Everyone runs to the football goal where they get trapped except for Kane 2 who didn't make it there in time. Max 2 tries to escape by flying through the net but it zaps him so they can't get out. Eagle Robot says that he can't be there himself but he has someone else coming for him. Suddenly, another Kane 3 appears and begins to rampage around the Castle. Kane 2 evolves into his own Kane 3 to fight him. Unfortunately, Tom's Kane 3 is losing. Everyone knows that he can only win if he evolves again. Tom starts to yell at him. The two Robots continue to fight but Tom's Kane 3 is running out of strength from eating too much. This just makes Tom even angrier. Everyone then starts to tunnel out of the goal they are in but there is a huge stone in the way. Jack's tag starts reacting again and he places it on the rock. It turns out to be Jack's Crest of Reliability and the group escapes through a tunnel. Tom realizes that Kane 3 will not evolve by himself and he decides to put himself in danger to make him do it. Tom then runs out into the middle of the Castle and tries to get the other Kane 3's attention. Yoko 2 and Bobby 2 evolve to try to help but Tom tells Kane 3 to evolve too. Suddenly, Tom's crest and Device begin to glow and Kane 3 however, Dark evolves to SkullKane. Everyone is very worried and confused about this huge Robot that Kane 2 became. SkullKane easily defeats evil Kane 3 but he then turns on Tom and his friends too. Yoko 3, Troy 3, and Max 3, who have joined in, can do nothing to stop the ultimate. He then continues on his rampage but suddenly runs out of energy and becomes Kane. Kane is very sorry for all of the damage he caused but everyone says that it is okay and not his fault. Tom take responsibility saying that because he had a crest, he thought that it meant that he had to fight by himself. Tom apologizes to everyone, especially Kane, who forgives him.

The Cruise Ship Captain

The youths continue to walk through the desert and are quite tired, considering it's hotter than ever. Though Tom is feeling guilty because of his mistake with Kane 2, Maria tries to make him feel better. After Tiffany 2 fantasizes about shading everyone from the sunlight, the group sees a large cactus that turns out to be nothing more than a mirage. They soon run into a hologram version of Gerard and inform him about their troubles with the Crests. He informs them, rather cryptically, that they have to have all the crests before any of their Robot can reach the Ultimate level. Suddenly a large cruise ship appears and heads straight for them. The group quickly boards, excited to get out of the sun. They freshen up, feast, and suntan aboard the luxury boat. However, the ship is run by Parrot Robot, a follower of Eagle Robot, who begins taking out the youths and their Robot, turning them to stone. The Pigeon Robots aid him in capturing the youths and Tom and Jack are captured, their Robots are the first to be petrified and Parrot Robot steals their crests and tags. He turns Troy 2, Max 2, and Terry into the stone next. When only the girls of the group and their Robots are left, they are forced to escape from their shower. Parrot informs the girls that their friends are baking out in the sun on the deck, and their Parrot counterparts have been turned to stone. Yoko 2 and Tiffany 2 both evolve and with little effort manage to defeat Parrot Robot. The robots are returned to normal and they, escape the ship. They think they've escaped until Parrot Robot, gravely injured, musters all his strength to steer the ship towards them through the desert. So the group hides behind a large cactus—one that isn't a mirage—which causes the ship to be catapulted into the distance, along with part of Eagle's Robot Dark Network. It then turns out that Maria's Crest of Sincerity is hidden on top of the cactus inside its flower, much to everyone's surprise.

The Dwarf Robot

After more walking through the desert and pondering the power of the newfound Crests, the group runs into the beetle robot, who they recognize from before, hiding underground. the beetle robot gets a hold of Tom, and all seems lost when Kane 2 hesitates to evolve due to lingering trauma from the incident with SkullKane. Tom rescues Kane 2 from the attacking beetle robot and they quickly find themselves in a tight situation—that is until the Dwarf robot rescues them in the knick of time. The dwarf robot is known for his tough training of other Robots and explains he has heard much about the youth and their Robots but is not impressed. He insists on training with them and informs Tom and Kane 2 that they will receive special training because they need it the most. The group decides to trust the strange Robot and he leads them to his hidden home through a secret doorway in the desert. They find themselves in a forest and see an Eagle robot behind them. The dwarf robot informs the worried youth that all the Eagle robot can see is the desert, so they are safe. They begin their long ascent up a huge hill to Dwarf's robot home, partly driven by the desire for food, and arrive to find that first they will be mopping the floors. While everyone else keeps busy, the Dwarf robot leads Tom and Kane 2 to a mysterious cave where they are told their task is to find a way back. That night they awake to find themselves on a small boat floating down a river and while wondering how they got there, Tom falls into the water and pulls Kane 2 in after him. When everybody is sleeping, Mark and Kevin's tags begin to glow. They head down the hill into the forest and the Dwarf robot spots them, informing the others of their departure the next morning. The girls joke around and claim that Jack will be the next one to disappear, causing him to accuse the Dwarf robot of their friends' mysterious disappearances. Meanwhile, Mark and Kevin continue searching for their Crests. Kevin wants to find his Crest so Max 2 can evolve, but Mark is hoping that he'll learn something about himself, and grow as a person when he finds his Crest. They are led to a well that is slightly outside Dwarf's hidden home. They find the Crest of Friendship and Crest of Knowledge inside the good walls, but because they are outside of the protected area Eagle robot detects the two of them and sends the Hyena robot to attack. They escape back into Dwarf's robot forest, but the Hyena robot breaks open the invisible shield hiding it. With the other Robot's power drained by Eagle's attack, their hope rests on Tom and Kane 2. Meanwhile, Tom and Kane 2 are still in the boat spinning down the strange river. They stop and appear on a bridge where Tom sees a younger version of himself trying to ride a bike. They help the young Tom ride his bike and he fades away into the distance. Tom and Kane 2 realize that the fear of Kane 2 evolving into SkullKane was keeping them from trying, similarly to the younger Tom not wanting to ride his bike because he was afraid he would fall. They understand that the task was all about overcoming their fears and escaping the "prison". Kane 2 evolves just in time to save the group and destroys

Hyena's robot and Eagle's robot Dark Network surrounds them. The youth thank the Dwarf robot for his help and return to their search for the remaining Crests.

45

The Prisoner of the Castle

The youth are busy examining a large generator of sorts that is attached to many wires spread across the land. Kevin believes it to be Eagle's doing. Kevin attaches the device to his own computer to find out that he might be able to access Eagle's network. He soon gets a message on his computer from a Robot in danger and claims he knows where the final Crests are. The group set off for where the Robot is being kept. Jack is rather indecisive about going but Kevin guides their way through the desert. Thomas's tag begins glowing and he soon receives the Crest of Hope from a rock wall. This means that Sarah's crest is the last to be found, which gives the Youth more motivation to save the captured Robot. In removing Thomas's crest from the wall, a tunnel is revealed and seems to be covered in some sort of Writing Amon. Kevin soon decides that the strange writing might actually be coding, like for a computer. He comes up with the hypothesis that everything around them might in fact be data. This causes discourse in the group as they don't know if they themselves are real or fake. Kevin soon calls up a map of the Amon World, and they discover it looks a lot like Earth. He enters the email of the Robot who sent the message to him and is able to pinpoint his location. Another holographic image of the Earth appears and it seems to match up almost identically to the map of the Amon World. He comes up with some more theories about their situation which eventually makes the group grow tired of all the complicated information. They are soon led by Kevin to an upside-down Castle where they see Eagle patrolling the outside. Kevin keeps preaching that the Amon World is a shadow of the real one, and they should try not to get hurt, even if they believe they are just data. Tom, Jack, Kevin, and Sarah make their way into the castle, using a secret back door to avoid Eagle and his guards outside. The group navigates through a series of secret passageways and eventually makes their way to the system's "castle wall", an electric fence. Tom is able to make it through without even looking back, as he has been convinced that he is only data. They arrive in a strange room and find the captured Robot, Smart Robot. He claims to be the webmaster of Eagle's network and the group decides to help free him from his prison. As they are partway through the multiple-step process of dismantling the prison walls, Eagle appears. All the Robot partners evolve to fend him off. During the battle with Eagle, the Smart robot escapes, taking Sarah and Yoko 2 with him. He escapes through another castle wall, and Tom follows. He is about to foolishly walk right through the wall and has to be held back by Jack. Kevin has to make him realize that his life in this world is in as much danger as in the Real World, due to the fact that they are linked. Tom panics and freezes, losing all the courage he previously had when he realizes he could be seriously injured, and lets the Smart robot getaway. Suddenly Mark and Maria appear with their Robot and force Tai to escape. Tom is in tears over his mistake and can do nothing but blame himself for not being able to rescue Sarah.

Defeating The Eagle Robot

Tom is still rather upset about his mistake, but the group tries to keep him positive. Kevin uses his computer and discovers that Sarah and Yoko 2 are still in the castle, which instantly raises Tom's spirits. Meanwhile, Sarah is trapped in a hidden room and the Smart robot begins to create a clone of her, which he plans to use to control her Device and Crest. This way, he can make Yoko 2 evolve and take revenge on the Eagle robot for imprisoning him. He also has the final Crest which he puts in Sarah's Tag. The group devises a plan to sneak inside the castle without being seen. Tom wants to be the one to save Sarah and receives the directions to the secret room from Kevin. He is scared to hear that he must pass through another electric fence, the thing that caused his last downfall. While Mark and Jack create a distraction, Tom and Kevin head into the castle through a secret passage. They take a few detours through the labyrinth inside the castle and are spotted by a security camera, however they didn't notice. Meanwhile, Maria leaves to help fend off the guards leaving Thomas alone. The Eagle robot attacks the Youth outside and easily defeats all of the Champion level partners. He then starts singing which causes them to evolve. One of Eagle's robot henchmen informs him that the remaining Youth is inside the castle. This brings him to the conclusion that Smart Robot must also still be there and while he is pondering this Maria, Jack, and Mark escape and return to Thomas. When Kevin and Max 3 are held up by an angry Eagle robot, it's left up to Tom to face his newest fear and pass through the upcoming castle wall. Kane's 2 encouraging words help him pass through the electric fence and his overwhelming courage causes his Crest to glow. He finds himself in Smart's robot hidden room, face to face with Sarah's clone. Tom then manages to steal Sarah's Crest back from the Smart robot. The smart robot opens up a hole in the floor underneath Sarah, but Tom is able to save her from falling and returns her Device and Crest. Yoko 2 is then able to evolve and Tom and Sarah then escape the castle along with Kevin and their partners. They meet up with the others as the castle collapses after being battered. Meanwhile, the Eagle robot has also found a Smart robot that deletes the clone of Sarah since it can't be of use to him without the Tag and Crest. The two of them plunge into Smart's robot expanding hole in the floor and into the heart of Eagle's robot Dark Network. Many of the Robots that were guarding the castle are sucked into the vacuum as the castle disintegrates. The smart robot is consumed, but the Eagle robot takes control of the huge ball of the Dark Network. He rises out of the castle, stronger than ever to face the youths outside. Kane 2, now Kane 3, takes on the Eagle robot with Tom by his side, but it isn't enough. Then Kane 3 evolves into Kane 4 because of Tom's courage and has no trouble defeating the evil Robot. However, destroying the heart of the Dark Network creates a dimensional rift, sucking both Tom and Kane 4 in. Tom and Kane find themselves back in the Real World, more specifically, in Tom's own neighborhood.

Tom Back to Real World

After defeating the Eagle robot, Tom and the now Kane find themselves back in the real world. Even so, Tom has trouble believing that he has finally returned. They arrive in a park Tom remembers from childhood and he realizes he is in his hometown, noting the familiar landmarks. They ask a little girl if she is real or fake, but just end up making her cry. Kane then begins attracting attention from people in the park, so they quickly leave. Tom gets excited when he realizes that he will finally be heading home. They arrive at the front door of his apartment and hesitantly go inside. Tom expects to see his parents, but soon realizes they're out of town. He raids the fridge and notices the calendar on the door. Though it has been weeks in the Amon World, in the real world it's the same day Tom left for camp. He comes to the conclusion that the time rift took them back in time (when really it is because very little time has passed in the real world during his absence). His younger sister Kate, who somehow instantly recognizes Kane, appears from her room and claims she's seen him before. Tom is confused by this and thinks she might be sick. He then calls the other Youth to see if they are home too but finds they are still stuck in the Amon world. Tom makes eggs for everyone and sees a news report about freak weather patterns around the globe. He thinks he's seeing Robot on the screen and Kate quickly assures him he is not the only one seeing them. Tom's Device begins acting up and Kevin's face appears on a nearby computer screen. Kevin warns Tom not to come back to the Amon World, saying he is better off where he is. Before Tom can get things straight, Kevin disappears, leaving Tom without a clue about what to do. Time passes and Kate tells Kane that he may never return home. Tom realizes that the Amon world's problems are slipping through the dimensions and affecting the real world. He wants to help but doesn't know how to return to the Amon world. He is about to lose his temper when the ground shakes and they see a Crocodile robot outside, firing at a nearby building. Tom decides to follow these mysteriously appearing robots in hopes of finding the dimensional rift back to the Amon world. He sees the Seal robot, who soon fades away, and then the Bear robot which Kane robot tries to fight. Kate chases after Tom and they both tell Kane robot he has to evolve. However, Kane's robot is unable because Tom's Device isn't responding. Kate and Tom's determination eventually activates the Device, allowing Kane to evolve. When he does, a rift opens in the sky. Kane 2 attacks Bear robot, knocking him into the rift. Kane 2 is sucked in next. Tom makes to follow, but Kate stops him, begging him not to leave her behind. She comes to realize that Tom has to go and holds his hand until the rift pulls him away. Little do they know, an eighth Device is sitting in their apartment, waiting for its owner.

The Bat Robot

Upon arriving back in the Amon World, Tom and Kane 2 find themselves in the exact place they were transported to the country and are surprised that the rest of the group is no longer there. Tom gets a signal on his Device and they follow it, hoping to run into one of their friends. They soon find Terry, who is on his own but has Thomas's Device and Crest. After Tom questions the whereabouts of Thomas, Terry tells Tom what has been going on ever since he left Amon World. Tom is surprised to find out he has been gone a lot longer than then the one day he spent in the Real World. Because time flows differently in the Amon World he has actually been gone for several months and in his absence, the team started to break up to search for him. Sarah was the first to depart on her own, followed by Kevin, then Jack, and then Maria, which left Mark and Thomas by themselves, but then the team falls apart, leaving no one to be found. Mark did his best to keep Thomas feeling alright about the split-up group while they continued their search for the others. They found an abandoned theme park and Mark decided to ride a swan-shaped boat around the nearby lake. He said he'd only be gone a few hours, but then weeks later he was still nowhere to be found, leaving Thomas and Terry all alone in the amusement park for several weeks. One day, a Robot named Bat Robot showed up, claiming to be a former servant of Eagle Robot, and told Thomas how he met Mark, who was supposedly glad to get away from him. Then Terry, doing his best to comfort his partner, lashed out at the "formerly" evil Robot, causing a falling out between him and Thomas Terry left on Thomas's orders and kept his Crest and Device safe while Thomas went off with Bat Robot. After Terry finishes updating Tom and Kane 2, they head for the amusement park, where they find Thomas who seemed to be upset about losing his partner. Thomas is overjoyed to see Tom again along with his Robot partner but they start to fight again. When Tom tries to comfort Thomas, the young boy asks to be Tom's little brother instead of Mark's, because Mark abandoned him. Bat Robot soon turns up with some "Carrots of Forgetfulness", which he got from some Rabbit Robot. He plans to have the group eat them, and they seemed thrilled that he has brought them food, seeing as they are quite hungry. Tom cooks the Carrots and when Kane 2 goes to the washroom and is warned by an unseen Sarah, hiding in the bushes, that the Mushrooms will cause them to lose their memories. Kane 2 arrives with the news of the poisoned carrots just in time to save Tom and Thomas from eating them. Bat Robot's plan is found out, and Terry and Thomas repair their friendship. Terry then evolves into Terry 2 to teach the deceiving Robot a lesson and after a battle through the amusement park, Bat Robot is defeated. Tom, Thomas, and their Robot partners then set off to find the rest of their team.

The Bad Restaurant

Mark and Troy 2 find themselves lost after traveling on a boat from the amusement park where they left Thomas, to whom they promised a quick return. They then follow some other Robot to a restaurant nearby. As they approach it, Bobby 2 gets thrown out the door by the slave-driving Duck Robot, landing right at the feet of Mark and Troy 2. They enter the kitchen of the restaurant to find Jack who is working off a meal he couldn't pay for. Mark fills Jack in and informs him that the whole group has split up. Jack tells Mark that Bat Robot led him to the restaurant where they ordered a large meal, but was unable to pay because he had 'Amon coins' instead of coins from the Real World. Jack explains how his work length has increased due to many silly accidents and his harsh boss. At first, he only had to work for three days, but he has worked himself up to over six weeks of payback time due to all the clumsy mishaps. Mark decides to help him work off the meal as suggested by the Pelican robot but realizes that Thomas must be worried about him. He tells Jack that he'll get Thomas and return to help. Before he leaves, the manager of the restaurant, Pelican Robot, who is being bribed by Bat Robot, blackmails Mark into staying. He claims that 'any accident can happen in the kitchen hinting that he might hurt Jack. Mark feels torn because he is worried about his little brother, but feels obligated to stay and protect Jack. He decides to stay for Jack's sake and reaches his boiling point when Jack continually questions him about Thomas He then apologizes for snapping and says they'll be done in no time because he is a great cook. Over many weeks, Jack causes more accidents and Mark has to do his best to keep his cool. Bat Robot also is trying to sabotage their work in order to keep Jack and Mark working longer and longer, and they are saved only by a sneaky Sarah who fixes the problems Bat Robot causes. Angered by the fact that she and Yoko 2 are messing with his plans, Bat Robot decides to approach Mark personally one night and turns him against Jack. Mark begs his boss to let him go find Thomas but is forced to stay. Not much later, Jack drops a plate because Bat Robot pushed him and Mark accuses him of screwing up on purpose just to make him stay longer. Mark storms off outside and at that moment, Tom and Thomas turn up and Jack explains the situation. Thomas reunites with his brother and Tom tells them they should get going, and quick. Mark says he doesn't want to leave, and he doesn't want to go anywhere with Jack anyway, complaining again that Jack is doing everything wrong on purpose. When Tom tries to intervene Mark lashes out at him too, claiming he's the reason they all got separated. Even Thomas is unable to calm his big brother down as his attempt to intervene is met with a harsh reprimand by Mark to be quiet. Then, the Pelican robot turns up, along with Bat Robot to attack the group. Kane 2 and Terry 2 chase after Bat Robot while Troy 3 and Bobby 3 try to take out the Pelican robot but it's not enough, considering the Robot's tough shell. Things get worse when Thomas is captured by the Duck robot. Jack does his best to save him but then gets captured himself. Mark, feeling touched by Jack's courage in saving Thomas despite how poorly he has been treating him, manages to activate his Crest of Friendship, which allows Troy 3 to evolve into Troy 4 for the first time. He quickly defeats the Pelican robot and scares the Duck robot away in an instant. Afterward, Mark apologizes for lashing out, and the four youths split up into two groups (Mark goes with Thomas and Jack goes with Tom) to follow separate readings on their Devices, hoping to find the rest of their team.

The Fox Robot

Kevin and Max 2, on a rocky path, on a journey to find Gerard, find themselves surrounded by signs warning them to turn back (as a trap set by Bat Robot to get Kevin's tag and crest for his master, Falcon Robot). The ground crumbles from underneath them, sending them into darkness. As he falls, Kevin hears a voice that accuses him of being greedy when it comes to knowledge and demands that he give up his curiosity. the voice demanded Kevin's "inner heart".) With no other options, Kevin gives in and enters a trance-like state. Moments later, he and Max 2 are floating through endless space, and the mystery voice reveals itself as the Big-brained Robot, Fox Robot, telling Kevin to forget everything. Max's 2 attempts to bring back the old Kevin fail as Kevin pushes him away and focuses more on Fox Robot's guidance and tutoring. Meanwhile, Bat Robot offers a piece of his curiosity to Fox Robot in exchange for Kevin's crest. Back in endless space, Max 2 catches Kevin's attention, who initially, angrily, shouts at him for interrupting his lesson. Max 2 reminds Kevin of the times they've had together, and Kevin snaps out of his dozy behavior, horrified at what he's done. After apologizing to Max 2, they then find their way into Fox Robot's storeroom where Kevin's curiosity is held, but not before Fox Robot discovers them and chases them back into his 'endless space' dimension, where a battle begins and Max 2 evolves up to the ultimate Max 3. He destroys Fox Robot's dimension and carries Kevin out of an enormous explosion back outside, where Mark, Troy, Thomas, and Terry are waiting for them.Meanwhile, Falcon Robot punishes Bat Robot for his failure by making him stay up in a cave.

The princess Maria

Tom, Jack, Kane 2, and Bobby 2 take Mark's swan boat to a large castle on an island. Upon entering, they find lots of Shrimps Robots, and Crabs Robots rushing around, running various errands for the "princess", who turns out to be none other than Maria. When Tom and Jack tell her she has to go, she reacts badly and has them all thrown out by her servant Robot. Tom and Jack wonder why these servants follow Maria's orders, and they take the group to their slumbering master, Frog Robot, who they say fell into deep despair after losing a fight contest, and will only awaken after seeing a fighter as good as the one that defeated him. They explain how Bat Robot told them about Mimi's amazing singing voice, so they found her and had her sing for them. The first time, Maria forgets the lyrics, so the Shrimps and Crabs serve her a food buffet to help her remember. The second time, she complains about the lack of decoration and asks for a makeover. She continues to make excuses and demand things from the Shrimps and Crabs, becoming spoiled and eventually not singing at all. Tom's first suggestion is that he sings instead of Maria, and everyone in the group ends up having a go, all failing miserably. Tom's next plan is to record Maria's singing on tape, with Tiffany's 2 help, though Maria quickly finds out, and has all five of them thrown in the castle dungeon. All five of them tell her off for how selfish she's acting but Maria couldn't care less. After having a bad dream where she is attacked by Falcon Robot, and no one wants to help her because of her selfishness, leaving her to fend for herself, Maria wakes to see Sarah, who comes out of hiding long enough to console Maria. Maria realizes what a fool she's been, and her crest glows as a result of her change of heart. She releases the group from jail and, after apologizing for how she acted, decides to sing again for the Shrimp and Crabs, much to their pleasure. When the Frog robot finally awakens to Maria's singing, he is less than pleased at being disturbed and blasts everyone with the horns on his back. He is eventually defeated by Kane 3, and Maria joins Tom and Jack as they set off to join the rest of the group.

The Gateway To Real World

The two groups reunite in a forest, where they begin wondering about Sarah. At that moment, their devices reveal her location, and they're on their way. When they're attacked by Bee Robots, Yoko 3 comes to the rescue. They then follow her to Sarah, who tries to run away but is caught between Tom and Mark. She's been hiding from the group to have some time to herself. It turns out that she can't get her Crest of Love to glow, because of a sad memory that made her believe her life was loveless. The group settles for the night, and Bat Robot attempts to attack Sarah in her sleep, but Yoko 2 takes the blow. Then Falcon Robot, the Robot that the Bat robot was working for, appears to take out the youths himself. His attacks finish off the Robot in seconds, and Yoko 3 tries to take him on but Sarah refuses to let her go. It's then that Sarah realizes her mother was trying to protect her and releases Yoko 3 to face Falcon Robot. When Yoko 3 is struck with a powerful blow from the Falcon Robot, Sarah yells out her love for Yoko 3, which allows her to evolve further into Yoko 4, who carries everyone to safety. Gerard appears to reveal that there is an eighth Youth and Falcon Robot who is already preparing to go to the real world to find him/her. The group decides to sneak into his castle. Kane 2 and Tiffany 2 go in disguise as recruits for the Falcon Robot army and are accepted for training by

Rooster Robot. The two, aided by Sam, Cole, and some Rooster Robot and Duck robots who are also part of Rooster's robot group of overworked henchmen, find a way in for the rest of the Youth by luring Rooster robot with soda. Meanwhile, Falcon Robot is about to depart for the real world through a Magic door, and the group finds him just as he's leaving. Falcon Robot escapes and sends Rooster Robot and his henchmen to fight the youth. After handily scaring off their enemies, the youth try to make their way to the door, but Cat Robot, one of Falcon's Robot most loyal servants, summons a horde of Vulture Robots. Their hypnosis creates such a diversion for the youth that the door closes before they can go through. With Cat Robot and Falcon Robot now in the human world, Tom beats on the door helplessly.

The Cards

With no idea of how they are going to open the door to the real world, the group is led by Gerard to his home. A searchlight guides the baffled youth down a staircase to the bottom of a lake where Gerard resides. There, they meet him face to face for the first time, rest, and go over the current situation. Gerard informs the youth that Falcon Robot has arrived in Real World. He then gives the youths ten cards with Robot on them, nine of which can be used to open the portal in Falcon's Robot castle, but only in the correct order. Though it seems as if the easiest solution would be to try all the arrangements of the cards, Gerard explains that this could take them to an alternate world of sorts and they really only have one shot to place the cards in the right order. That night Kevin is up late talking to Gerard about the two worlds, the real world, and the Amon World. He explains to Kevin that robots have attributes and are sorted into Data, viruses, and Vaccines, and because he has no attributes, he is not technically considered a Robot. The next day, the group sets off with the cards and Kevin's laptop, newly modified by Gerard. They raid Falcon Robot's castle, and with him and his best servants gone, getting to the door is easy. Max 4 fights off the last of the guards and the group began working on figuring out the order of the cards. The different youths have different ideas of how they are sorted, by level, size, and even alphabetical order. In the confusion, everyone decides that Tom should be the one to make the decision about the order of the cards. After being encouraged by the other Youth, Tom elects Kevin to decipher the code. By using the information Gerard gave him, along with the upgrades on his computer, Kevin quickly figures out the pattern. However, for one space there are still two cards left, Bobby's 2 cards and Kane's 2, with only one being the right one (Gerard accidentally mixed one in). Kevin then leaves it to Tom to decide which card is the right one. When Spider Robot, one of Falcon's Robot servants, attacks, Tom must decide quickly which card is the right one while the Robot fight off the hordes of enemies and the pillar that Falcon's Robot castle rests on crumbles more and more with every passing moment. Just by luck, he chooses Bobby's 2 cards, opening the door and taking the group into the real world just as Troy 4 defeats Spider Robot and the pillar finally topples. They arrive back at camp, delighted to realize they have made it back safely with their Robot in tow, and head off to find the eighth Youth.

Return To Real World

After just barely making it through the doorway that Falcon Robot entered, the group finds themselves back at their camp, now with their Robot, just mere minutes after the freak snowstorm which preceded their departure for the Amon World. It feels as though weeks have passed which baffles the youth, but they understand that time flows differently in the two worlds. Disguising their Robot as stuffed toys they found on a mountain path, the group meets with their teacher who tells the youth to pack up their belongings. They learn camp has been closed due to the snow and they are being returned home. After weaseling their way out of a conversation involving their Robot the group meets up with the other camp youths waiting by the buses. The Robot partners are shocked to learn that there are millions of other youths around the world. The Youth then persuade their teacher to drop them off, and after Tom's begging, Thomas's sad, and Jack pointing out his responsibility their teacher agrees to the youth's wishes. The youth find out that their Devices are still working in the real world. Their teacher is equally interested after grabbing one out of the youth's hands. Tom fears that the adult might break it but soon learns there is nothing to fear. Meanwhile, Cat Robot is on the prowl with a Tag and Crest, looking for the eighth Champion. Falcon Robot is impatiently waiting in a secret hideout and is not pleased to hear the champion has not turned up. He reveals that he has created many copies of the eighth champion's Crest, but only he has the original. After the youth find their way to Place, they soon discover that they all used to live there at the same time. They try to make a conclusion about the strange coincidence but must escape when some of Falcon's Robot henchmen appear. An Elephant Robot, one of Falcon's Robot destructive recruits is soon spotted across town and is running amuck. The youth are far enough away that they don't hear him, and continue on their nostalgic journey. When the group is contemplating their connection, Jack points out that although he didn't know Kevin at the time, he seems to know why Kevin moved after living in the condo complex for only six months. Just as he is about to reveal why he is interrupted by the passing of several police cruisers responding to an emergency. The rampaging Elephant Robot approaches and Yoko 2 evolves to Yoko 3 and later Yoko 4 to face him. As the battle ensues, Thomas. is the first to be reminded of a similar battle that happened when they all lived in the area. The other youth soon remember the battle too, remembering it was between Kane and a bird-like Robot, but after the fight, they disappeared. When Elephant Robot is defeated, the group concludes that they were chosen as the Champions after witnessing a Robot battle at place four years ago. They also conclude that the eighth Champions must have also witnessed that same battle. After fleeing from approaching Police emergency vehicles coming to investigate the aftermath of the battle, the youth agrees to search for and find the eighth champion before Falcon Robot can.

The Squid Robot

Bat Robot is talking with Falcon Robot and explains that Yoko 4 was spotted in town along with the seven youth. He explains that they have not yet found the eighth Champion, but they are still looking harder than ever all around the city, and he probably will be found soon. Falcon Robot then tells Bat Robot that he has to make sure the seven Youths do not find the eighth champion. Meanwhile, the group decides to travel home on the subway. After a bit of confusion, Kevin finds the quickest (though complicated) route to the city. They buy their tickets and once again tell their Robot to try to avoid public attention by not talking or moving. Right before the subway arrives, Kane and Troy jump on the train tracks ready to attack, thinking the train is an evil Robot. On the subway, Sarah offers her seat to a mother and her baby. The baby then begins pulling on the appendage in the middle of Yoko's hair and continues to do so until she finally yells at him to stop. Most of the people on the subway are quite shocked, but Sarah pretends that she was just using ventriloquism to make the 'doll' talk. This impresses the people, and a boy begins asking his father for his own 'Yoko doll'. Sarah tells the boy's father where to buy one and he and the boy leave at the next stop, as most of the passengers follow them. Everyone falls asleep, not having slept properly in a while and when they awaken, they find out they missed the stop they were going to transfer at. Unfortunately, Terry was going to wake them up but Tiffany reminded him that they were supposed to stay quiet, so he didn't say anything. Before the group transfers trains, they decide to have a bite to eat, because they are all very hungry and their Robot might need to evolve. While looking for a place to eat in the crowded subway stations, Kevin and Jack get separated from everyone else. Kevin then discovers that their Devices aren't working properly, so they cannot track the other's locations. They exit the subway station to look for their friends and almost cross paths with one of Falcon's Robot henchmen, a large, mysterious figure in a trench coat. Jack sees the rest of the group through a window in a tall building and can tell they are eating without him and Kevin. They quickly meet up with the rest of the group to find out that there is no money left for them to order any food. Kevin realizes his Device is working again and guesses it probably only works from close distances in the real world. After eating, the youths decide that they should attempt hitch-hiking home because they don't have money for the subway and it's better than walking. Tom tries to stop a car first with no luck and tells Mark to try next, but he appears to be too embarrassed to do it. Jack and Kevin go next, which amuses the others, and they stop a taxi. The driver then realizes the youths don't have any money and leaves. Sarah and Maria then coincidentally end up stopping Sarah's "red pigeon" cousin, Daniel who gives them a ride. A news report comes on the radio in the car about the incident from earlier. Kane then makes a mess in Daniel's car as they are going over a bridge. Everyone piles out of the car, and Sarah's cousin loses his temper. He gets mad at Sarah, who wanted to take the blame for the others, and then starts to blame Jack, despite him having nothing to do with it. Daniel then accidentally knocks Kevin over the bridge, and as he is falling towards the water, Max evolves to Max 2 just in time to save him. Unbeknown to them, swimming in the water below is one of Falcon's robot sea henchmen, Squid Robot, a giant monster. Daniel gets scared and leaves, while Bobby 2 evolves into Bobby 3 to take on the evil Robot in the water. The fight between the two attracts a lot of attention from bystanders and Squid Robot is easily defeated. The Youth manage to escape unnoticed from the crowds of people watching the fight. Bobby 3 then takes the Youth to City, by traveling in the river. Unfortunately, little did they know, Bat Robot saw them, and is now aware of their location.

The Eighth Device

In his secret location, somewhere in City, Falcon robot is angered to hear from Bat Robot that the youth has already defeated two of his henchmen, Elephant Robot and Squid Robot. Meanwhile, Tom is on his way home, when he begins to wonder if his little sister Kate might be the eighth champion, because she also witnessed the events at City four years ago, just like the other Champions. Kate's parents arrive home and when she goes to greet them, the family cat Ziko is curiously sniffing the Device under her bed. When Tom arrives home, he is very happy to see his parents, much to their surprise, and quite emotional, too. Kevin returns home and lets Max into his apartment through his bedroom window, so his mom doesn't see. Confident his parents will never understand their situation, Kevin goes to get a lock to keep his parents from entering his bedroom. He then has a flashback of overhearing his parents discussing whether or not it's time to reveal to him that he was adopted. Kevin takes his dinner to his room to share with Max, while Tom does the same with Kane. Tom asks Kate if she has seen a Device. When she says no, Tom shows her his. It turns out that Ziko has in fact taken the eighth Device, and is traveling with it in a lorry to another location. The Device starts reacting when the truck goes over a bridge. A silhouetted Robot is seen with one of Falcon's Robot Crests, which is glowing. Bat Robot is also nearby with one of the copied Crests, and it's glowing, too. Later that night, Kevin is checking out some modifications Gerard made to his computer when he finds a map of the City with an alert message from Gerard saying that an unidentified Robot is lurking in City Bay and he's the only one of the Champion who's still awake. Alarmed, he wakes a sleeping Max. After Kevin calls the other Champion at home to confirm that they're all asleep, He and Max quickly whip up a disguise for the latter and take a cab down to the bay and begin tracking down another one of Falcon's Robot henchmen. They find Fish Robot, the creature from the water. As a battle ensues, Kevin gets a signal from the eighth Device and decides to follow it by himself. However, Bat Robot is also following a signal from the Device, which Ziko abandons, and finds Kevin. Max 3, fresh from defeating Fish Robot in an intense battle, comes to the rescue just in time, while the eighth Device is carried away by a crow. Kevin returns home to his quite worried parents and overhears them talking. They are concerned that he has changed since he returned home from camp, and are worried he is hiding something. Meanwhile, Tom gets a signal from the eighth Device, when it is really just the crow flying overhead with it. Falcon Robot, as vampires do, travels through the midnight, looking for fresh blood from young people. Meanwhile, battles between strange-looking monsters are reported on the news, as Tom looks for his address book. He fails to find it but meets everyone at the park anyway. Kevin tells them of his discoveries late last night and asks that they all try to get in contact with people in their address books. So, everyone splits up to begin the mission of finding the eighth champion. Sarah and Maria end up taking a break in the air-conditioned City Tower, as an intense heat wave is passing over the city, but Aluminum Robot, another of Falcon's Robot's evil henchmen, follows them in. Soon enough, a battle begins, and Tom and Kevin notice from about a mile away. They arrive, and Kane 2 evolves to his Ultimate form to defeat Aluminum Robot. While all this is happening, Cat Robot encounters Kate and begins to suspect her as the eighth champion. However, she hesitates to attack as planned and retreats out of Kate's residence in confusion.

Eighth champion

It seems that Deer Robot and Sheep Robot are among the Robot that has entered the real world. They are having a night in the town, riding around in taxis and watching all the people. Meanwhile, Mark is taking Thomas home on the subway. Troy has to explain to Terry that even though Mark and Thomas are brothers they live with different parents and in different parts of the city. Mark wants to ensure that he gets Thomas all the way home despite his younger brother not being so keen on the idea. Terry then comments on how close the two siblings are, despite living apart. However, Thomas takes it the wrong way and yells at him, causing him to fly off at the next stop. After Mark and an indecisive Thomas get off the train to look for him, they walk all around town while Mark scolds Thomas for yelling at Terry, and eventually, they run into the two mischievous servants of Falcon Robot, Deer Robot, and Sheep Robot. They had just gotten thrown out of what appeared to be a casino and then ran into a teenage girl. Everyone thinks they are two children in costumes but Mark and Thomas can easily see that they are not. Troy evolves, only to find that the devious pair is just playing around. They hide from the raging teenager that they angered earlier and then explain that they aren't really evil. They then jump on top of a street light and cause a car accident. Forced to run from the police, the group flees the scene ending up in the window display of a clothing store. They spot Terry while playing dress up but he quickly flies away. Next, Deer Robot and Sheep Robot then steal some ice cream to cheer Mark and Thomas up but end up running away from the shop owner they stole it from. Falcon Robot then appears and learns that his two minions have been messing around instead of looking for the eighth Champion. Falcon Robot orders them to steal the boys' Crests and a chase ensues. When Mark and Thomas are cornered, the two supposedly evil Robots admit that once again they just want to have fun and weren't planning to take their Crests. The two Robots just want to hang out. Falcon Robot is unimpressed that they let the boys get away and banishes them to his dungeon in the Amon World, but not without putting up a fight. Troy 3 then evolves to Troy 4 in order to avenge Deer Robot and Sheep's Robot's unfair punishment. Meanwhile, Terry's 2 anger has subsided, and he is searching for Thomas at the park, mainly because he heard two girls talking about it earlier. When he notices the battle between the two powerful Robots he realizes Thomas is in danger. He evolves to Terry 3 and with Troy's 4 help, weakens Falcon Robot, causing him to retreat. Thomas is in tears while apologizing to Terry 2 they make their way back through the streets towards the subway, reminiscing about their short-lived friendship with Deer Robot and Sheep Robot. Meanwhile, Cat Robot is watching Kate, who she still suspects is the eighth champion, and is planning to take her out the next time she approaches her. Cat Robot is still struggling to approach Kate, and wonders why this could be, thinking back to how she tried to attack her before, but couldn't bring herself to do it and ran off. She thinks about the past, remembering how badly Falcon Robot first treated her, even looking at one of the scars she still bore from his punishments on the back of her paw. At that moment, Wizard Robot, a good servant and friend to Cat Robot, appears, to remind her of a time when she helped him in the desert, a memory she seems to have forgotten. He then suggests that the reason she struggles to attack Kate is that she is her Robot, making her the eighth chosen Robot. At that moment, Kate appears on the nearby balcony, and Wizard Robot takes this chance to bring the two together. He then gives Kate her Device, which he recovered earlier from a bird's nest while luring off Bat Robot when he came snooping, confirming her status as the eighth champion. When Tom sees them all outside, his first reaction is to attack, but he realizes his mistake when Cat Robot saves Kate from Kane's 2 Fire Breath (not meant for Kate of course). Later, Wizard Robot and Cat Robot set off to pick up Kate's Crest in Falcon Robot's hideout, and soon run into him. Falcon Robot realizes the situation, and throws Wizard Robot into the nearby river, taking Cat Robot as bait to draw out the eighth champion.

The Cat Robot

Fog (caused by the Falcon robot) begins to spread around City, rendering all forms of digital communication and public transport in the area useless. The next morning, a horde of Ghost Robots led by Red Ghost appears to round up residents into Big Sight where Falcon Robot is holding Cat Robot captive. Amongst the people captured are Maria, Tiffany, and Sarah. Sarah remembers how she and Jack defeated Ghost Robots in her last encounter, using intimidating chants. So, she explains her idea and the people begin fighting back against the Ghost Robots. When Leopard Robot appears and hope seems lost, Tiffany 3 evolves to Tiffany 4 to neutralize his evil intentions. Yoko 3 also shows up, evolving to scare Red Ghost and the Ghost Robots away. Meanwhile, Tom and Kate have met up with Mark in a nearby location, where he is updated on Kate's new status as the eighth champion. At that point, Falcon Robot decides he's had enough and takes on Tiffany 4 himself. Tiffany 4 fails to defeat Falcon Robot and has to be taken away by Yoko 4 who flees with Sarah. Meanwhile, Tom decides that he must help the others, leaving Kate with Mark, and Kevin, back in his bedroom, succeeds in setting up a Robot Barrier against the Ghost Robot to protect his parents while revealing Max to them, then going off to investigate the source of Falcon Robot's fog. Thomas runs into Jack at the harbor across the river, and Bobby 2 evolves into Bobby 3 to take them to the other side. Tom and Sarah run into each other. After Tom tells her where to find Mark and they split up again so Tom can get to the convention center, Jack and Thomas soon run into Sea Snake Robot, who attacks them and sends Jack and Thomas. flying into the water. When Jack sacrifices himself to keep Thomas afloat, his Crest of Reliability glows, and Bobby 3 evolves to Bobby 4, who saves Jack and Thomas and defeats Sea Snake Robot, before finding Wizardmon in the water, holding Kate's tag and crest. At the communications tower, Kevin runs into Mark's dad, while Red Ghost has followed Yoko 4 to Kate's location, where she gives herself up in order to spare the others' lives, unable to bear watching their Robot get overwhelmed by Red Ghost and his own backup. As Kate is taken away, Mark feels like he's let everyone down. Sarah tries to calm him down, and they head for the communications tower, where Kate is. Meanwhile, Jack and Thomas find out about Kate and Cat Robot's true identity from Wizard Robot, and soon also arrive at the communications tower. After Wizard Robot restores Tiffany 4 from her paralyzed state, the group begins their assault on Falcon Robot in the tower. Their attempts at beating him fail, even when Tom shows up to help having rescued Maria from the Convention Center. Wizard Robot successfully delivers the Crest of Light, but Bat Robot intercepts the Device. Things begin to look up when Terry 2 evolves toTerry 3, who destroys Red Ghost and actually manages to hurt Falcon Robot, but Falcon Robot fires at Kate and Cat Robot, and Wizard Robot takes the full blow. As Cat Robot mourns over the loss of her best friend, Kate's Device reacts, forcing Bat Robot to drop it.

Tom throws Kate's Device to her, allowing Cat Robot to evolve into Cat 2, who focuses the rest of the Robot's attack power into a single shot, wiping out Falcon Robot. Just as everyone begins to celebrate, they realize that something isn't right, as Falcon Robot's fog still looms.

The Super Falcon Robot

Despite Falcon Robot's apparent defeat, his fog barrier continues to loom over the district even thicker than before. As everyone tries to decide on the next course of action, Kevin receives an incoming message on his laptop from Gerard, who claims to have found a way of defeating Falcon Robot once and for all. He then shows them an ancient prophecy describing a sky darkened by many falcons, the rising of a king, and a miracle at the hands of angels, but it only confuses the youth. In the meantime, their thoughts turn to their families, so the youth set off to find them and make sure they're okay. At his house, Jack finds only his brother Justin, who's been hiding in a closet, but cannot find his parents. Once Jack returns, the group decides to split up, with one portion going to the convention center and the other trying to find a way through the thickening fog barrier. Jack and his brother Justin arrive at the convention center first, giving them a brief chance to talk about Jack's future career as a doctor, which seems to be something that Jack's father wants, rather than Jack himself. Their discussion is cut short as the others begin to arrive. After clearing the convention center of Falcon Robot's minions, the youth find their parents, in a deep sleep with the rest of the people from the district. Nothing seems to wake them up. Justin takes the opportunity to finish the conversation from earlier, telling Jack that he should be aiming for what he wants in life, even if his father doesn't approve. On the water, the other group, consisting of Booby 2, Terry 2, Mark, Thomas, and their father Henry, can find no way through the fog. They head back to the shore, only to be ambushed by a pack. Retreating back to the nearby van only worsens things, as the Robot tip the van on its side. Just when it seems like there's no way out, the Robot mysteriously vanishes, the only clue to their disappearance being a cloud of falcons—the first part of the ancient prophecy. Back at the convention center, Kevin's parents are also taking the opportunity to talk to Kevin, and decide to reveal the truth concerning Kevin's adoption, which he had long been in denial about. Kevin also confesses how his obsession with computers came as a result of this denial. By the end of the conversation, Kevin and his parents seem closer than ever before. Max 2, who was watching nearby, is tearfully touched because of this. Meanwhile, the people in the convention center suddenly begin chanting Falcon Robot's name, and the Bat Robot is reminded of Gerard's prophecy. From it, they conclude that Falcon Robot will reveal his true form at nine seconds and nine minutes past 9:00—"the hour of the evil" (9:09:09). This gives the group mere minutes to make their way back to the TV station, where a cloud of falcons are gathering. A flash of light and the collapse of the TV station reveal the beast that is Super Falcon Robot. Kane 2 and Bobby 2 are quick to react and evolve to their Champion forms. It's soon obvious that this isn't enough, as they're met by a strong opposing wind and Bat Robot's taunting words. However, Bat Robot soon pays the price for his evil actions and is betrayed and consumed by his own master. Realizing that they need more power, Kane 3 and Troy 3 evolve to their Ultimate forms. Kane 4 and Troy 4 manage to at least hold Super Falcon off, as Henry, Tom, and Mark rush back to the convention center to evacuate everyone. Of course, they soon face the truth that they'll never get everyone away in time, leaving them with only one option—to fight. Cat 2 is first to suggest this, though insists that only she and Terry 2 go. So the two evolve to their angelic forms and soon join the fight. Super Falcon drains Kane 4 and Troy 4 of their energy, and they revert back to their Rookie forms. Meanwhile, Kevin continues to study the rest of the prophecy, and the message soon becomes clear—Terry 3 and Cat 3 must fire arrows of Lightning and Thunder at Mark and Tom. Of course, this seems like an odd solution, but by this point, the group is willing to try almost anything. So, Tom and Mark brace themselves as the angel Robot prepares to shoot. The arrows strike, and a flash of light is emitted from the two Champions, causing Kane 4 and Troy 4 to react, as they're thrust into a new type of evolution, sending them past the Champion and Ultimate stages, and onto the Mega stage—Kane 5 and Troy 5 are the resulting miracles. With newfound strength, the two Mega Robots begin taking on Super Falcon Robot. Things seem to be going well until Super Falcon is cut open to reveal a powerful energy source, which pushes the Robot away. But at that point, the youths' crests shoot beams of light, binding Super Falcon, and giving Kane 5 and Troy 5 a clear shot at the weak point—Super Falcon is finally defeated. As things begin to return to normal, everyone's relieved, until the vanishing fog reveals something even stranger in the night sky. It's an upsidedown image of the familiar landmass that Kevin later identifies as the Amon

World, showing that while the Youth have been fighting Super Falcon for only a few days, centuries have passed in the Amon World, revealing that something is terribly wrong. After rescuing a plane damaged by the image in the sky, the youth decide to head back to Amon World right away to investigate and sort the problem out. Now they must face an evil that can bring forth more destruction and darkness than even Super Falcon.

The Evil Masters

Through a telescope in the Amon World, the Evil Masters observe the events unfolding on Earth, preparing for the arrival of the Youth. Meanwhile, the Youth arrive to find the Amon World in darkness and soon find Chris hiding in the tall grass nearby. He explains how he was separated from his best friend Steve, and how the world was scrambled up into a single spot called Red Mountain, where the Evil Masters rule. Seconds later, one of the Evil Masters, Red Crocodile Robot, shows up. All the Robots evolve to their Champion forms but they could not overpower the Mega Robot and are sent spiraling into unfamiliar surroundings when Red Crocodile uses his Sea of Power. The Youth soon find themselves in a location covered in complete darkness. Terry 3 goes to investigate but gets attacked and reverts to his rookie form. Red Tiger, another Evil Master reveals himself, and the Robot evolves to their Ultimate level. They have been beaten once again and using his Red Cannon attack, Red Tiger sends the Youth and their partners to yet another completely dark location. While in the midst of falling into the endless darkness, the group suddenly stops moving and Troy 4 and Yoko 4 start fighting one another against their will. Everyone starts moving uncontrollably and Kevin is the first to notice they are acting like string puppets. It is then revealed that they are all being controlled by Red Fox, another Evil Master. He uses his Magic Stick Attack, forcing the Robot to de-evolve, and sends them to yet another location, an outdoor arena. Red Lion, leader of the Evil Masters, turns up and easily defeats Kane 4 and Troy 4 in their Mega forms, Kane 5 and Troy 5. He then decides to take each champion out one by one, starting with Maria but Chris takes the blow and gets deleted. All hope seems lost until Peter Robot whisks the Youth to safety in his invisible bubble. Before leaving, Peter informed the Youth that simply being together is not going to be enough to win this battle, and they will have to figure this one out themselves. He tells them their next step should be to climb Red Mountain. Peter then sends the Youth to safety and does his best to keep the Evil Masters from pursuing the Champions.

The Scorpion Robot

The group is forced to watch the Evil Masters' arena explodes with Peter inside as they escape in the forcefield he created. They then find themselves on a familiar beach they visited at the beginning of their adventure. Everyone seems to be quite down about both the loss of their friend and the fact that they haven't really made much progress if they are on the same beach they started on. While trying to figure out if their whole journey has been pointless or not they hear someone yelling for help in the water. Thomas and Kate are eager to help the creature so all the Youth take a rowing boat to where the splashing's coming from. The drowning Robot turns out to be Shell Robot, very likely the same one they fought on their first day in the Amon World. The Robot manages to beat Shell Robot in their Rookie forms, leading the team to believe they've become a lot stronger. Tom remembers that Kane 2 had to be at the Champion level to defeat the evil Robot last time. Though everyone else seems doubtful, Tom wants to believe that their partners are stronger, and everyone agrees after explaining that getting stronger is what Peter wanted for them. The fog on the beach suddenly clears and the now completely worn-out group heads for a snack bar nearby. While rushing to the stand, Jack and Maria trip and aren't able to enter the shack. This turns out to be a good thing, though, because the snack shack is actually a trap set by Scorpion Robot, one of Red Crocodile's henchmen. He attacks them, covering them in the sand and causing them to pass out. Luckily, because Jack, Maria, and their Robot avoid the trap, they are able to sneak up on Red Crocodile, who is talking with Scorpion Robot. Red Crocodile notices that two of the Youth are missing inside the restaurant and orders his henchman to find them. Scorpion Robot chases after the remaining Champions and their partners, but they easily outrun him because he ate a load of clams. He retreats into the water and when he reappears Tiffany 2 and Bobby 2 are ready to take him on. He's finally defeated when he gets distracted by some more clams, allowing the Champion level Digimon to evolve to their Ultimate forms. Tom and the others start to regain consciousness inside the building. Maria, Jack, and their partners enter the building and have to wake up everyone to ensure their safe escape. Red Crocodile begins to burn the shack, thinking the Youth are inside; it turns out the only occupant of the building was an unconscious Scorpion Robot, who catches fire and rushes out into the water. Angered that his servant has failed him, Red Crocodile lifts Scorpion Robot up high into the air and drops him to his death. The Champions are now safe, but Jack doubts Tom's claims that their partners are getting stronger because it took two Ultimate levels Robot just to take on one of the Evil Masters' flunkies. A red Crocodile approaches the Youth on the beach, and they are forced to escape into the water nearby. Tiffany 4 attempts to fight him off to no avail. Red Crocodile strikes her with his tail, causing her to de-evolve to Tiffany 3. While the group is safely situated on Bobby 4, Red Crocodile disappears into the water, then attacks, causing Bobby 4 to de-evolve to Bobby 3 and knocking the rest of the group into the water. They are now powerless, and the Evil Master prepares to finish them off.

Defeating Red Crocodile

All hope seems lost for the kids, until Whale Robot shows up, ambushing Crocodile Robot and carrying them away. Minutes later, Crocodile Robot begins a search with a group of Lobster Robots, while Whale Robot finds a distant island where the Youth can rest. After everyone attempts to fish on the island, Bobby 2 hears of some nearby Lobster Robots from a school of fish and they're soon on the run. Whale Robot escapes by swimming to an area of high pressure in the ocean where the Lobster Robots cannot follow, but Crocodile Robot catches up. When Whale surfaces near a coast, Kane 4 evolves to Kane 5 in order to fight Crocodile Robot while Bobby 4 destroys the Lobster Robots. While the other Robot defends the Youth, Crocodile Robot attempts to crush Kane 5 in his jaws. Kane 5 escapes Crocodile Robot's grip when Whale Robot rams him. Whale Robot is then destroyed by Crocodile Robot, just before Kane 5 finishes him off by drilling through him. With the Evil Master destroyed, the ocean begins to reassemble itself, and the group decides what to do next. Tom is ready to move on, unaware that everybody else is coming to terms with the loss of some good Robot allies. After a while, they head into the nearby forest, and into Fo Robot's territory. Shortly after entering Fo Robot's forest, Kate begins hearing a sound that apparently no one else can hear, though Tom just tells her to stay with the rest of the group. Fox Robot instantly begins dragging them to his mansion in the forest on a hidden conveyer belt, so the group hides in the trees. However, he splits them up using identical figurines on a special map. After he's done messing around with them, he approaches Thomas and Mark, who are without their Robot. Thomas agrees to 'play' with Fox Robot so that Mark is spared, and after a game of hide-and-seek in Fox Robot's mansion, Thomas manages to trick him so he can explore his mansion a bit more. Meanwhile, Stork Robot, one of Fox Robot's servants, is holding up the others from rescuing Thomas, but he is easily destroyed by Yoko 3, causing Mark to turn on Sarah because Thomas could have been found with Stork Robot. Thomas finds Fox Robot's map of the forest and remote control for the conveyer belts, amongst other things, and he destroys it all. He then escapes the mansion and finds the others. When Thomas was being praised by Tom and the others, Mark changes his expression, from relieved to sad, and leaves the group without any explanation. When Fox Robot sees that some of his toys, the ones used to control the Champions, are destroyed, he vows he'll get revenge on Thomas.

The Turtle Robot

Mark, who's been having trouble interacting with others in the group, leaves them quietly while they're busy praising Thomas for outsmarting Fox Robot. The group notices he is gone and is becoming quite concerned about his whereabouts when Jack speaks up to tell them that Mark is not in danger, but rather he just left on his own. They realize that he has been acting strange lately and decide to go look for him. Just before they set off, Kate hears a strange voice that no one else seems to hear. Meanwhile, Mark settles down by a lake, where he tries to figure out what his problem is. He is upset because he doesn't have a purpose in the group now that everyone else has seemed to change for the better while he is still the same. He figures that to change like the others, he has to do it by himself. Turtle Robot, a wise Robot working under Fox Robot, approaches Mark with a secret plan to make him turn against the others. At first, Troy 2 seems defensive while Mark just plain doesn't want anything to do with him. Turtle Robot says he knows why Mark is upset and explains that he can help him. This intrigues Mark and he falls into Turtle Robot's plan and looks into the nearby lake. Instead of his reflection, he sees Tom's face. Turtle Robot explains that it means Tom is the one preventing Mark from reaching his full potential. At first Mark suspects, it's a joke but the evil Robot convinces him otherwise. The rest of the group is wandering through the forest, having no lead as to where Mark is because of their non-responsive Devices. They find Fox Robot and come under attack by a group of Monkey Robot. Maria is quite stubborn about running away but the group escapes. After a bit of a struggle, most of the Money Robots are beaten by the group's Robot at the Champion level. A few remaining Monkey Robots attack Maria so Tiffany 3 evolves into Tiffany 4 to protect her. Kane 2 then evolves to Kane 3 to fight them off and Fox Robot runs off in annoyance. Back at the lake, Mark is convinced by Turtle Robot that deep down he knows he doesn't have any friends. He begins to feel hopeless and indecisive, so Troy 4 tries to reach out to him and says he'll stick by him no matter what, and that they are friends. This causes Mark's Crest to activate and Troy 4 warp evolves to Troy 5. Mark makes up his mind and they set off to fight Tom. Turtle Robot reports back to Fox Robot about the plan in action and warns him that the Champions have something he doesn't. This causes Fox Robot to lash out in anger, destroying Turtle Robot. In the forest, the last of the Monkey Robots is attempting to suck the group into his garbage can, until Troy 5 appears to destroy him just in time. Just when everybody – especially Tom and Kane – try to greet Mark, Troy 5 attacks, challenging Kane. Everyone is in disbelief at his behavior and shocked at why Mark would be doing this.

Champions reunite again

Mark confronts Tom, angry about what Turtle Robot told him, and gets Troy 5 to attack Kane, which forces him to warp evolve to Kane 5 in order to protect Tom. An unstoppable battle begins between the Mega Robots, and much to the other Youth's dismay, Tom and Mark start lashing out at each other as well, with Tom claiming he's only doing it for all the sacrifices others have made for the group. This pleases Fox Robot greatly, who is watching from a distance. The other Robot looks on helplessly, knowing that they stand no chance against two Mega Robot. As a result, some of the Robots start arguing leading to more discord within the group. Meanwhile, Kate discovers some kind of presence nearby and begins to converse with the mysterious entity, which has been trying to communicate with her for a while now. It tells Kate to raise up her Crest of Light, so she does, emitting a blinding light, and taking in the entire group. This halts the fighting and reverts the Mega Robots back to their In-Training forms. They then appear in a familiar location, City, where the mystery is being spoken to them through Kate. The group is told of how they were chosen as the Champions after witnessing a battle between Good Robots and Evil Robots four years ago. The mysterious being that is possessing Kate explains that 'it' is similar to the Robot, in that it is made up of data, but unlike the Robot, it cannot take a physical shape. Kate is the only one with which it can communicate them. The Youths kid about how young they look while flying over the buildings. While Tom and Kate are on the street near Robot, the other Youths are all on the balconies of adjacent buildings. Jack is seen on the phone and Markand Thomas are shown together, obviously before their parents divorced. The being then takes them to a room where hooded people control the balance between good and evil in the Amon World, and the youths' future Robots are in their Robots-Eggs. Attached to the Robot-Eggs are the respective Crests and Devices. They watch events from the past that are digitally animated into the present, like ghost images. The being possessing Kate explains that they took the information they got from scanning the youths four years ago to make the Devices and Crests. She explains that Tom and Kate were chosen because they helped the Good Robot evolve during the fight, and the other youths have a connection and are also very special. It is revealed that the Crests were made from the strongest qualities the youths had when they were scanned, and if they lose the quality the Robot may become corrupted (like the evil Robot did). Suddenly, the youths watch as the location is attacked by an evil robot. The group watched as the evil robot attacks the people, and steals the eight Crests connected to the robot's egg. Because they are just images of the past, there is nothing the youths can do. They then witness a younger Gerard rescuing the robots Eggs and taking them to Fork Island (losing Cat's Robot-Egg on the way due to being chased), where they await the arrival of the Champions. When the group arrives back in the forest, Kate is back to herself again. Mark, still shaken up from the fight, leaves the others, even though he has his answer to why they were chosen, saying he needs some time to himself. Sarah suggests they split up into two groups but Mark is against the idea. Maria then also decides to leave the group, because she doesn't want to fight anymore, or see anyone get hurt, so Jack decides to stay with her, so she is not alone. cat robot stays hopeful, pointing out that they are the Champions and are destined to reunite again.

Defeating Red Fox

The bear robot is being chased by the Wood robot when a meteor crashes right on top of him. This attracts the attention of Maria and Jack as well as Tom's group. Tom immediately wants to investigate the meteor, but Thomas suggests going to Fox robot's mansion instead. When the group is unable to decide what to do, Kevin suggests a vote. Sarah notices that Tom hasn't voted, who is wondering how Mark would vote and has taken it upon himself to look after Thomas in Mark's absence. He finally decides to check out Fox robot's mansion, but not to look for trouble. Sarah expresses doubt, but Tom comforts her by saying that he won't let anyone get hurt. Meanwhile, as Iron eagle rises from the meteor, Jack and Maria discover Bear's robot, who was injured during his fall. Although Jack wants to leave, Maria immediately takes charge and tends to the Bear robot. Fox robot then appears and Bobby 3 evolves to Bobby 4. Because Maria hesitated to let Tiffany 2 join the fight, Fox robot quickly defeats him, but before he can finish him off, Iron eagle appears. Fox robot becomes annoyed and the two Megas begin fighting. Seeing their chance to escape, Jack and the others run away. They seek shelter under a tree and Bear robot promises to repay their kindness, as per his code of honor. When Maria asks why he fights the Lion robot, the Bear robot says its destiny. When Maria questions that and says he should have a greater purpose in life, the Bear robot becomes upset. Iron eagle robot, no longer fighting Fox robot, then discovers them and they run for a new hiding place. As they're taking cover, the Super lion appears and the Bear robot prepares to fight. Tom's group arrives at the Fox robot's mansion. Although Tom initially wants to look around himself, the others convince him to allow them to join him. They attack two of the Fox robot's playmates, the Deer robot and Zebra robot, thinking that they are guards. The two Robots admit, however, that they dislike Fox robots and offer to show them around the mansion. Upon entering, they discover various dangerous toys. When Fox robot returns from fighting Iron Eagle, the group fires at him with one of his own cannons. Fox robot realizes that it's the Champions and prepares to attack. Super Lion takes Maria, Jack, and the Bear robot to a place near the restaurant where Jack was forced to work once. Meanwhile, the Fox robot attacks Tom, Sarah, Kevin, Thomas, and Kate with an army of ducks, which are defeated. Eventually, the Robot evolves to its strongest form and fights the Fox robot, gaining the advantage. However, the Fox robot brings his mansion to life and it attacks them. Iron Eagle finds Maria, Jack, and Lion robot, who evolves into the Super lion and fights the Iron eagle. During the fight, Iron eagle shoots an energy blast at Maria, which the Super lion takes to save her. Bobby 4 dents the Iron robot's armor with his hammer, allowing Super lion to finish him off by impaling him with his claw. In the forest, Mark and Troy 5 appear, confronting Fox's robot and easily destroying him, causing the forest part of Red Mountain to disappear. After the battle, Mark and Troy 5 leave. Meanwhile, the Lion robot ends up being deleted as well, but not before making peace with his rival, the Bear robot.

Red Tiger appear

Tom's group is crossing a desert when Kate collapses in the heat from sickness, The others manage to put her under a bench with some shade. Tom begins to get upset and has flashbacks to a time he and Kate were younger. Max 3 flies them to a nearby city, and Kevin uses his laptop to locate a pharmacy where they can find medicine. This proves a drastic mistake, however, as Red Tiger is given their location every time they plug the laptop in. Red Tiger sends his Robot minions out to all the locations in which the pharmacies were found. Meanwhile, after finding a pharmacy, Kevin plugs in his computer yet again to find the best specific medicine for Kate, still unknowingly, giving Red Tiger his exact location. They find the medicine, only to be ambushed by Red Tiger's army. Kevin and Tom manage to escape, but Tom loses control in impatience and snaps at Kevin. He feels responsible for his sister, and he reminisces of another time his sister was sick. Tom was much younger, as was Kate. All he wanted to do was play soccer, despite being told to watch his sister at home because she was ill. Focusing just on himself, but not wanting to leave his little sister alone, he brought her along to the park where he wanted to kick a soccer ball around with her. He began to get frustrated that she can't kick it well, and tried to teach her. Not long after, she collapsed, and an ambulance came.

Tom was harshly scolded by his mother because Kate nearly died of pneumonia. When Kate came home, she apologized to Tom for not being able to kick the ball right. Tom took the lesson to heart and decided to look after Kate from that point on. After Tom calms down, they at last figure out they were being tracked by the computer systems. Kevin quickly adjusts the program so they cannot find them, but this only causes Red Tiger to order "Operation 1": having Red Crow and Blue Crow destroy the whole city to flush out the Champions. Fearing the worst, Tom and Kevin meet back up with Sarah, Thomas, and Kate, who escaped the building they hid in before Red Crow could destroy it. Unfortunately, Red Tiger arrives, forcing the group to hide in a nearby building. Sneering that the chase is part of the fun of a hunt, Red Tiger destroys the building, and the Champions fall into a deep void...

Defeating Red Tiger

Right after Kate wakes up and is back to health, Sarah and Yoko 3 as well as Terry 2 show up, where Thomas and Cat 2 have been taking care of Kate. Sarah also hands Kate the medicine that they found, which Tom must have dropped when they became separated. While exploring the underground labyrinth of sewer tunnels, Sarah, Kate, and Thomas come across a large group of Rats Robots enslaved by Dog Robot, who is working under Red Tiger. The Numemon is powering the vast city above from the sewers. Kate wants to help free them and begins to glow with a mysterious light. She rescues them and they praise her as 'Queen Kate'. Sarah, Thomas, and their Robot are busy trying to fight off Dog Robot with no luck as their Robot can not seem to evolve. They barely escape after he gets his hand stuck in a wall, and find themselves amongst the worshiping Rats Robots. Suddenly Dog Robot appears and the Rats Robot tries to fight him off, with no luck, and just as he is about to finish them off, Kate faints again as the youth Robot is empowered and evolves. They battle for a while until he is scared away and Kari begins to glow once more, pointing the group in the direction of the others. Meanwhile, Dog Robot reports back to Red Tiger and tells him that he fought with the Champions, but was defeated by a young, powerful girl. Red Tiger is displeased with his efforts and kills him. Tom and Kevin are exploring the sewers when Tom gets angry at Kevin and their tired Robot. He wants to continue looking for his sister while the others want to rest. When an annoyed Kevin tells Tom to stop bossing them around, Tom lashes out at Kevin, pins him on the ground, and punches him in the face. In the midst of the fight, Tom hears someone approaching. They continue to fight (but they are only pretending) and hide from view, awaiting the mysterious figure. Their Robot attempted to evolve but their energies were too low. This causes Tom to apologize to the understanding Kevin about hurting him and Iron Robot, the person they could hear coming, approaches. They had previously met on Fork Island and Iron Robot is now leading a resistance against Red Tiger and vows to help the youth safe. Tom and Kevin are relieved to see a friendly face and ask if he has seen the other Champions close by. Iron Robot, surprised to hear that Tom and 'Queen Kate' are related, informs them that she and the others are headed in their direction when suddenly Red Tiger appears. After the two groups reunite, the evil Robot corners them and battles with Iron Robot. Birdramon, Iron Robot, and Cat 3 help him fight too, but the Mega-level Robot is too strong for them. They appear to be beaten so Kate offers herself up to be eliminated first by Red Tiger. Before he can strike, however, the hordes of Rats Robots swarm over Red Tiger in order to protect their Queen. It is of no avail, however, as Red Tiger swiftly kills every one of them. The deaths of the Rats Robots spurs the light in Kate further, and it powers Kane 4 enough to warp evolve. With his power amplified to an unbelievable level, Kane 5 brutally slices Red Tiger with his Weapons Destroyers, and before he can strike back, he falls to pieces. With Red Tiger defeated, his city begins to disappear. The Champions decide to erect a small shrine to honor the Rats Robots. With the other Evil Masters destroyed, Tom and the others head off to the top of Red Mountain, now ready to face Red Lion.

The Spider Robot

Jack and Maria, along with the friends they've collected, watch as Tiger Robot's city dissolves. As they continue on, Maria becomes tired, so the Frog robots, Fish robots, and Ice robots look for food. As they're resting, Jack remembers that his brother, James, told him that he didn't have to become a doctor if he didn't want to. He resolves to become a stronger and better person, rather than one that always screws up. When the group continues on, they arrive at a colorless and broken Primary Village. Hearing a harmonica, the group rushes toward the sound, thinking that it is Mark. When they find the source, however, they realize that it's the Raccoon robot, who has become depressed. They ask him to join their group and when he hears that Terry robot and Thomas have been fighting as well, he agrees. Jack asks the Raccoon robot where he got the harmonica and they are able to determine that Mark crossed the nearby lake with a swan boat. Jack decides to leave Maria with the friends they have gathered in order to search for Mark, feeling that he must go alone to find where he fits in the group. Jack says that Mark was looking for the same thing and he wants to know if he found it. Bobby 2 says that if Jack feels strongly about this, then it must be the right thing to do.

Meanwhile, after making a marker for the Rat's robots that died against Red Tiger, Tom's group continues up Red

Mountain until Sarah spots the Lion robot's hideout. The Spider robot offers to take care of the Champions for Red Lion and attacks. Kane evolves to Kane 2 but is easily defeated. Terry 2, Yoko 2, and Max 2 all evolve to Champion while Cat 2 evolves to Cat 3. The battle continues (with the Iron robot also aiding the Champions), but the Spider robot seems to have an advantage as she easily deflects all attacks made on him. Kane 3 urges Tom to let him warp evolve, but Tom refuses, saying that he needs to stay in reserve. When Kevin uses the Robot Analyzer on the Spider robot, Tom begins to look at the big picture and realizes the seriousness of the situation. He asks Sarah and Thomas to find Mark, knowing that they need to plan ahead to avoid more innocent deaths and to defeat the strongest of the Evil Masters. Yoko 3 and Terry 3 leave the battle to help Sarah and Thomas in their search, leaving Max 3 and Cat 3 to fight the Spider robot. Max 3 evolves to Max 4 to help Cat 3, but the battle between her and the Spider robot seems to have become personal. While the youth are uneasily watching the catfight, Kate is very passionate about supporting Cat 3. Cat 3 destroys the Spider robot, but their brief celebration is cut short when Red Lion arrives. Kane 4 warp evolves to Kane 5, but Tom knows that everyone is needed for this battle.

Defeating Red Lion

Wandering down a dark cave, Mark begins to despair and feels that he has been a poor brother and friend. Despite Troy's 2 protests, Mark thinks that Tom is better at being a brother to Thomas than he ever was. Mark tells Troy 2 to go away and dismisses him. Troy 2 bites Mark on the leg to get his attention and says that if he really wants him to go, he will, but Mark tells him to stay. Mark then says that he's always felt alone and that after his parents divorced, he pushed people away and wouldn't let anyone see him cry. Due to Troy's 2 companions, Mark begins to see that he isn't alone after all and that he does have friends. Mark and Troy 2 promise to be best friends forever. The cave around them dissolves and they are almost immediately spotted by Jack, who has been searching for them. Jack returns Mark's harmonica. Sarah and Thomas find Mark's boat. Sarah begins to doubt herself and the same darkness that had a hold of Mark grabs her and she falls into a cave with Yoko 2. Just then, Jack and Mark find Thomas and he tells them what has happened. They go into the cave, with Mark warning them not to be scared. Upon finding Sarah, Mark and Jack try to bring her out of her depression. They give her the confidence to keep going and tell her that they came to the Amon World for a reason. Sarah realizes that this is true and the cave around them disappears. They rejoin Tom and his group to find Kane 5 badly injured.

Mark tends to Tom, who is also hurt, and says that their friendship always meant a lot to him. Tom says that he never stopped believing in him and Mark's crest glows, healing Kane 5. Troy 4 then Warp evolves to Troy 5 and joins the fight against Red Lion. Troy 5 returns and fighting alongside Kane 5 they take on Red Lion. After some tricky attacks from the Hell Lion, both Mega Robot seem to have the upper hand in the fight. Just as everyone else is about to evolve, Red Lion pulls out a white cloth and the confused Champions don't know what to think of it. He quickly throws the cloth which grows into a huge sheet that covers the Mega Robot. Tom and Mark are covered with a sheet when they run to their partners. Red Lion then removes the sheets to show that they have seemingly "disappeared". He then reveals that they have been turned into key chain figurines. The other youths try to run away while the Iron robot holds him off but he too gets turned into a figurine. The only way the group is able to escape is by using trapezes placed over a large chasm. As they attempt this, Jack, Kevin, and Max 2 are captured. While the rest hide terrified, Rd Lion stalks them in a sadistic game of hiding and seek. When Red Lion attacks, Yoko 4 and Cat 3 hold him off to give the others time but are captured and transfigured into figurines. Once finding temporary safety, Sarah charges Thomas to take Kate and run. Thomas, Kate, Terry 2, and Bobby 2 start to flee the area, however, Bobby 2 decides to stay with Sarah to fight back. She tells him, he stands no chance against the Red lion and to help Thomas and Kate, along with Terry 2. As Bobby 2 reluctantly turns to leave, Red Lion bursts into the passageway from the floor. As he brags that they will all become part of his collection, Bobby 2 snatches the figurine of Mark and throws it to Sarah, who throws it to Thomas and is then turned into a "doll" herself. Thomas, Kate, and Terry 2 escape through the door at the end of the corridor, while Bobby 2 (of the screen) is turned into a figurine himself. As the rest of the group has fallen prey to Red Lion's demonic abilities, the only ones left are Thomas, Kate, and Terry 2. While the two of the remaining youth try to escape up a rope, Rd Lion catches up to them and Terry 2 evolves into Terry 3 to try to fight him off. Unfortunately, he is easily defeated and Red Lion then cuts the rope, climbing after the two youth. When Red Lion attempts to take Thomas, Kate grabs onto Thomas, despite Thomas imploring her to let him go for her own safety. Kate refuses to let him go, so Red Lion cuts the rope further, causing Thomas and Kate to fall. As they fall, Thomas clutches the keychain form of Mark and after hearing the encouraging words of his older brother, he is reminded that hope remains. His Crest begins to glow and Terry 3 finally evolves into Terry 4, who catches the two falling youth and places them safely on the ground. He flies up to deal with Red Lion, who throws a sheet at the former. The archangel slices the sheet in two and delivers a single slash to Red Lion using his Excalibur sword. He recovers the keychains and sends Red Lion hurtling away, seemingly to death.Terry 4 then returns every key chain to the Robots and Humans they once were using his "Light Sword" ability. They think it's all over until Red Lion resurfaces with hundreds of robot soldiers. Just then, Maria and Tiffany 4 arrive with an army composed of the Robot the youth had earlier befriended. The partner Robot evolves to their highest forms and, alongside their allies, fights back against the robot soldiers. After they've been softened up, Terry 4 opens his "Gate of Hell" to suck in the robot soldiers horde, at which point Kane 5 and Troy 5 corner Red Lion and blast him into the void as well, defeating him for good, causing the last remnant of Red Mountain to disappear. The reinforcements Maria brought along return home. As the light begins to return to the world, Kevin gets a message from Gerard telling them that the Evil Masters were never the real enemy and that the real enemy is the one who created the Evil Masters. Just then, the ground shakes, the sky grows dark and the Champions soon realize that the fight is not over.

Defeating Robot A

The Champions fall into darkness before stopping in midair. Gerard then contacts them and tells them of an ancient evil that the original Champions defeated and that a similar evil has returned and created the Evil Masters. The connection is broken and Robot A appears. He reveals that he was created from the pain and suffering that is caused when Robot attempts to evolve but ended up disappearing. He says he hates the Champions for being able to be happy when he is forced to be miserable and attacks them using the abilities of the enemies that they've defeated in the past, such as the Evil Masters, Dragon robot, and Bat robot. Robot A then uses "Reverse evolve" to return all the Robots to Rookie-level (with the exception of Cat Robot). When the Robot attempt to evolve again, Robot A destroys the Champions youth's Crests. The youths begin to lose confidence and Robot A uses that fear against them to trap them and their Robot in a binary prison in the world of delusion. The youths begin to lose hope, but their Robot encourages them, reminding them of all the apparently unbeatable odds they overcame. They all realize that they've grown up and become stronger, better people, and the symbols of their Crests begin to glow over their hearts. They realize that they never needed the Crests and that they had the power inside them all along. Their Robot all evolve to their highest levels. They are then capable of reassembling themselves before Robot A, who reacts in shock and disbelief that they escaped the Delusion World, and prepare for the final battle. This scene begins with the last few scenes of the previous scene including the segment of Crests, evolutions, and returning to Robot A, who is in shock and disbelief that the Champions were able to escape the Delusion World and return to the Amon World, and worse, enable their Robots to evolve when he had destroyed their Tags and Crests. The team attacks him with all their might, with Kane 5 and Troy 5 going for his humanoid body while the Ultimate Robot destroys the arms of the core. Seeing he is about to be defeated, Robot A, in one last ditch effort, begins to detonate his body to "restart" the Amon World, using his suicidal attack Total Annihilation attack. The Champions begin to doubt that they can win, but their Devices begin to glow and shoot out lasers that create a box around Robot A, preventing his eruption from destroying anyone but himself. With Robot A defeated, the Champions prepare to spend the rest of their summer in the Amon World, after taking a group shot with all of their Robot allies. However, Gerard informs them that they either had to leave immediately or remain in the Amon World forever, now that they have two hours left before the Amon Gate closes, due to the time between the Amon World and Earth having now become synchronized. After saying their good-byes to their partners—with Kate giving Cat Robot her whistle and saying that she is sure that they will meet again—except for Maria because Tiffany hides so she doesn't have to say goodbye, the youths depart for home, with Maria upset because of Tiffany, but as the trolley—the same one from the Amon World—begins to leave, Tiffany, after some persuasion by the Iron robot, comes out and says her goodbye to Maria while running alongside the trolley. The other Robots soon join her and send off their friends, and the Champions ride into the Gate. To end the adventure, Tom states that even though this adventure is over, for now, the gate can't stay closed forever. He's sure that this won't be the last time they see the Robot.